ARC CITY STORIES

ARC CITY STORIES

TODD CINANI

J. L. AARNE

DAVENE LE GRANGE

PATRICK TILLETT

MAX MCCAMISH

TRACY CROSS

AVA SILURIAN

AMBER BENBOW

BLKDOG

www.blkdogpublishing.com

SCARLET 1

MIDNIGHT ON THE MIDWAY 17

BROADCAST 2220 49

NEO(N) BUSHIDO 81

GETTING CLEAN 103

LAYERS 123

REGRET ME NOT 153

FELK THE NETWORK 169

SCARLET II 195

PLAYLIST 213

SCARLET

By Todd Cinani.

Lights from the holo-ads and glowing buildings reflected off her red air bike as she sped between the towers. Maneuvering deftly above, below or around slower traffic, flying over and under sky bridges crossing between the buildings and their sky walkways—Scarlet could have let the bike drive itself, but it erred on the side of safety and she was running late for her delivery. She preferred to drive anyway, especially when she was in a rush: she liked the adrenalin. The heads-up display in her eye ran a countdown for required delivery time and showed the best route. She trusted the route display and barely worried about the actual address. After all, the upgrade had cost enough.

Upgrading had become a bit of an addiction for Scarlet, compulsively snagging the best cybernetics and software codes money could buy. For this reason, she only occasionally took legal courier jobs, and those just to keep her license in order. Most of her jobs were either barely legal or downright illegal. Those were the jobs that paid, and they paid well. Like the current delivery: a small metallic cube. What was in it, she didn't know and did not care to know. That was why she was reliable, that and her on-time delivery record. This one was going to be close, but she'd make it.

She weaved on the bike, zipping and darting on the plane of the horizon, until a 90-degree upward pivot pointed her toward corporate housing with a sickening and thrilling lurch. As she made the maneuver, hanging on tight against acceleration and gravity, speeding straight away from the ground, a call came in on the heads-up display. She saw Beetle's round hairless head pop into her eye. He was one of her Finders, who set her up with jobs. His specialty was finding things for people, and one of those things was couriers who didn't advertise to the general public and kept their mouths shut.

"S'up, Beetle? Short on time."

"Scar, when are you ever late?" He asked with a smile.

"Never, but no time for you now. Call you after I finish."

"Make sure you do. I have a great jo…"

Scarlet cut him off. He'd always had great jobs before, but lately his jobs had been getting worse with low pay and greater risk. Not many high pay for the risk jobs coming from him. She slowed the bike and leveled it off again. The buildings still glowed but there were fewer holo-ads cluttering the night sky in the higher-level corporate housing areas. The blinking icon on her display signified that she had reached the/her destination. She hovered over the port dock and lowered the bike next to a luxury sedan. Grabbing the cube out of the compartment behind her, she hopped off the bike, stretching out in the full-body armor that fit her svelte form. A bulge on each hip housed her guns; a compartment flush against her back held additional offensive and defensive gadgets. At her level work was dangerous, and being over-prepared was better than being under-prepared. Her helmet receded into her armor, exposing a mane of fiery red hair, glowing bright blue eyes over a sharp, predatory nose, and alabaster skin. Despite being entirely a combination of cybernetics and bio augmentation, the effect was both stunning and a bit frightful.

Scarlet signaled to the customer that she had arrived, and recorded the exact time of arrival in the cyber node implanted in her brain stem.

A door in the wall slid open and a large man in a suit came out: obviously security. He threw up a holo-clock between them and gave her a stern look. She threw up her stamped arrival time. He shrugged and both holographs disappeared. She held out the cube at the same time he sent the credits to her account. He took the cube and retreated the way he had come. She had already verified the funds in her account, and was moving them into various accounts at other institutions as she got back onto the bike. The helmet closed over her head once more.

The bike hovered off the dock, and Scarlet put it in a nosedive back to the less sterilized levels. She pulled back up at level 162, once again darting and weaving in and out of air traffic. She had two more deliveries to make, both regulars and less critical. She arrived in one of the many entertainment areas with large sky walks for pedestrians and more traffic. She slowed down, sent the destination to the bike and let it drive. Delivery was not due for a few hours and she knew the receiver, so no rush. The last delivery was not due at all: it was a favor.

Eventually the bike arrived at the destination; a dock at one of many mostly empty docking pads. It was still a bit early for the clubbing crowd. Scarlet again reached behind her, opened the storage compartment in the bike and pulled out a flat metal object. She hopped off the bike, retracted the helmet and walked to the entrance of Donny's club, a virtual holo-club with themes that transformed your image to fit with its ever-changing backgrounds. As she opened the door and entered the first-floor bar, Scarlet slid virtually into the persona of an ancient western Gun Slinger. Looking down at her new image, Scarlet bemusedly wondered what foolishness could be had on the upper floors. She really had no use for clubbing, so thus far had only seen the first floor, mainly delivering Donny his shipments.

She instantly noticed the group of Horizon Riders, or Hot Heads, or whatever the current slang for them was, sitting in a corner to her left. They were taking the new Event Horizon drug: part nano-bot, part stimulant, part who knew what else, it overclocked a user's node and body, bringing with it euphoria and sensations of invincibility. Problem was eventually it made users cyber-psychos who'd rampage until the cops put them down. Scarlet figured these guys were not far from that: their movements were sped-up like a film fast-forwarded, a bit jerky as if their muscles could not keep up with the signals they were receiving. She'd keep an eye on them.

Scarlet went to the bar and sat next to the only other customer. He looked like a western traveling salesman, dusty from the road. The bartender came up and whipped the bar in front of her. He had a handlebar mustache, greasy slicked back hair, a black vest and wrinkled white shirt with arm garters on it. A holo-person; damn, she had no use for them.

"And what would the lady like this evening?"

"Whiskey, neat and tell Donny I'm here. After that get lost." Scarlet had already let Donny know and time stamped her delivery, but why not fuck with a holo and give him some useless tasks? The bartender went to the door behind the bar and yelled for Donny. Meanwhile a glass of whiskey appeared from the bar box that had risen as soon as she placed her order. She took a sip.

"I'm not sure that's a sipping drink," the salesman-looking guy next to her said.

"I like to make things last," she replied with a smirk.

"Dexter." He extended his hand which she took.

"Scarlet." They shook. "And what bring you to the ancient west, Dexter?"

"Work, always work. I'm a finder and I'm looking for a person for this big corp guy. So far no luck," Dexter said with a sigh.

"Can't help you there, I'm just in delivery."

"Courier, eh? I guess you work with other Finders, huh?"

"Yeah, a few. Not the brightest but they get me the jobs that pay."

"Well if you need an upgrade in talent here's my card." He threw up a holo-card which she recorded and filed.

"Thanks. I may do so."

"Well with that I have to mosey, as they say in the ancient west. Guy I'm looking for has to be around here somewhere." He touched his virtual hat to indicate his leave. "Oh, before I go, watch out for those Hot Heads in the corner."

"Tagged and recorded as soon as I walked in," Scarlet responded. "I guess I'll see you on the trail, partner," she added sarcastically. He gave a slight bow and headed toward the door.

Donny came in from the door behind the bar, looking stressed and exhausted. "Sorry Scarlet. Shit I'm trying to fix."

"Donny, what the fuck?" Scarlet asks gesturing about the bar.

"Yeah, I know. My holo service is screwing me. Starts out with Outer Space, Jungles, Moroccan palaces and what not, now I got the ancient west as a greeter. You know what level two is? The fucking Victorian era. No one wants to dance and party in the least fun era civilization has ever seen."

"Sounds rough."

"Yeah, I'm about to break contract if they can't

give me what I want. Either that or go outta business."

"Well anyway, here's your gear." Scarlet slid the thin box over to him.

"Thanks." He sent the credits, and Scarlet once again transferred them into multiple accounts.

"Hey, you may want to watch those guys in the corner," she advised.

"Yeah, saw them earlier. One thing I have that works is a new security system. Any suspected violence and cannons pop out of the ceiling and lay waste."

"Good to hear it. Well, I best be going. Adios, partner." Scarlet smirked and tipped her virtual hat. With that she headed to the door.

Back on her bike, Scarlet had one last drop for the night: the favor. She zipped straight down 17 levels and causally joined traffic. She sent the destination to the bike and let it drive. She really only liked driving when she had to beat the clock. The bike docked adjacent to a street restaurant. She hopped off and pulled a large burlap sack out of a saddle compartment. The compartment closed and locked as she headed into the restaurant and took a seat at the bar. A large man in a turban and apron came over to greet her.

"Scarlet! Mon amie," the man said with a smile. "What do you have for me today?"

"I don't know Michel, wild mushrooms, herbs…" Scarlet tossed him the sack. "…stuff from your list."

Michel began rooting through the sack with the occasional squeal of glee. It all came from the wilds beyond the wall, from some scattered farms of people who decided to flee the city and live off the land. Most didn't make it because few knew how to survive anymore, and there was no longer any data on the subject. At some point a trader on the fringe came through with an old book about agriculture and farming. An enterprising woman bought it and made copies, which she then sold at exorbitant prices. Some bought it and took the risk. Even with the book, most could not make it. The book was about farming, not survival, and you had to survive before you could farm. But there were a few who were able to do well, and they traded food for parts they needed to cobble together farm equipment. It was all black market, but no one much cared what happened on the fringe. The wealthy would always look the other way for some fresh tomatoes and other luxuries. Scarlet imported some of it; the one agreement she had was that she would keep a sack for herself. She personally had no use for it because she could not cook and had no idea what most of it was, so she gave it to Michel who would make magic with it. Michel in turn fed her for free.

"And what would you like to dine on tonight?"

"Surprise me," Scarlet responded.

Michel went back into the kitchen with the sack and came out with a bowl of steaming stew and a glass of wine. It wasn't real wine of course. It was just alcohol, water and flavoring but she'd never had real wine so she thought it was good. Vineyards no longer existed, even beyond the walls. There were rumors of hydroponic vineyards for the corporate elite, but those were just rumors.

Scarlet dove into the stew and eyes widened with joy. "I love you, Michel…" she said under her breath and continued eating. Michel had real meat in the stew. Not stem-cell generated chunks of meat-like-stuff, but actual meat. She had only tasted real meat once before, here at Michel's. She realized that she would remember that taste for the rest of her life. Where Michel got the meat from and what kind of animal it was Scarlet didn't care. Wherever, whatever… it was a thousand times better than vat meat.

After eating Scarlet sat and savored her meal for a while before calling Beetle back. Beetle's bulbous head popped into the heads-up in her eye. "So what's the job?" she asked, to the point.

"It pays well, let me just say that first off. 5000

credits."

"5000C is not well, it is moderate, but go on."

"Well it's 5k to deliver a bit of black-market tech to some sketchy geezers on 75."

"You know I don't go below 78, so no deal."

"It's a piece of piss, Scar. Just drop the thing off, you're 5000C richer for it. Take you an hour maybe."

"I don't go below 78, and I'd rather not even go that low, and definitely not for 5000C." Scarlet had risen up through the levels, through the horror and filth and skull-crushing depression. She could remember how, not far below 75, the mold and fungus fucking eats people who don't keep moving; she'd seen it. Once she was clear, she decided never to go below 78 again, no matter what the pay was.

"It's a quick job, please Scar." She could see the obvious stress on his face.

"I like you Beetle, but no."

"Scar, the shite has gotta get there by ten tomorrow or I'm in trouble, bang in trouble." He was panicky now.

"You got in over your head again, didn't you Beetle? Made promises before you had everything lined up, didn't you?" Scarlet stated more than asked. "I'd love to bail you out again, but you know my policy. Why'd you even take a job that low?

"A bit of risk for reward." He stammered.

"Get someone else. Conrad's good. He's from the lower levels like me, and not afraid of a fight."

"He's not as good as you, Scar."

"He's good enough for your *easy* job and he doesn't mind the lower levels. For 5000C, he'll jump at it."

"Yeah, maybe you're right. I'll give him a call." Scarlet could see the sudden wheels turning. Maybe if Conrad would jump at 5000C, he'd be happy to do it for 4000C.

"Alright Beetle. Got anything else?"

"Not at the mo."

"Call me when you have something above 78."

With that she ended the call, got up, waved to Michel and headed back to the bike.

***

Scarlet walked into her apartment. Compared to others, hers was quite luxurious. It still only had two rooms; a bedroom and a main room with a kitchen attached. The kitchen was wasted space which she had thought of converting but never got around to it. The furniture was elegant and comfortable, and a large round window looked out at the glowing city. The bedroom was much the same. As she entered, Fenris padded up to her. Fenris was her great wolf. The wolf had been code bonded to be her companion and was her protector as well as guardian of the apartment. She rubbed his forehead and took off her suit. Before going to the bedroom to put on some comfortable pants and a light shirt, she made a drink on the kitchen bar and went to sit in a large chair under the window. Risky jobs paid very well. That's how she could afford her place, the armor, the bike and all her many upgrades.

Scarlet glanced at a framed photo on the little table next to her lounge chair. It was of a little girl with jet black hair, dark skin and shabby clothes staring innocently at the camera. It was a reminder of who she was, where she came from, and that she was still a human being somewhere deep down inside her. Over the years, as she began to earn credits, she began to alter herself. At first, it was just little cybernetic upgrades to help her perform better. Eventually it became an obsession to the point where between cyber upgrades and bio augmentation there was very little of that girl left. Unfortunately, the price was a growing dehumanization: a lack of empathy and inability to maintain a romantic relationship. She had men she liked and had sexual relationships with, but she could never come close to love. She wasn't even sure what love was. There was Christopher though. He was a Net Flyer. He could hack anything He was the one who created her banking system to enable her to hide her illegal earnings in multiple accounts, making the transactions look legal. He recoded Fenris. He was her longest relationship and it lasted a year but like all the others she sabotaged it once it was apparent he was in love with her.

Scarlet had become something else; at the same time more than human and less than human. That little girl who rose up through the levels changed with every venture upwards to become something like a cold demigod. The more credits the more she invested in her godlike status, replacing this, upgrading that until she would become superhuman and not have to worry about anything. She would also continue to rise up the levels in housing to larger more luxurious apartments. That seemed to be her only goals. Shallow, true, but what else was there to hope for but a better, more powerful existence?

There was a knock at the door. Fenris growled from his position at her feet. She used her heads-up to see who was on the other side. A well-groomed man stood in an expensive suit; a corporate executive, she thought, high ranking. But where were the guards? She used the camera to scan up and down the corridor, no guards. She focused on the man again and scanned him. No weapons. Curious, she thought. Fenris padded up to the door with a low growl.

Scarlet sent the open-door signal without leaving the chair she was reclining in. The man in the doorway jumped, seeing that it was Fenris who greeted him. Fenris gave him a guttural growl, teeth barred. After a moment the suit regained his composure and looked past Fenris to Scarlet, comfortable in her seat holding her drink. "Uh, Miss Scarlet? I'm sorry, I don't have a last name."

"It's just Scarlet for now. Where are your guards?"

"They are waiting downstairs." He smiled. "I did not want to appear aggressive. May I come in?"

"What do you think, Fenris? Shall we let the suit in our private abode?" Fenris growled some more fangs still barred.

"Nice, what is that, a wolf?" the suit asked. "Must have cost quite a bit."

"He was a gift from a satisfied customer." In truth, she'd taken Fenris in lieu of payment, because she was instantly attached upon seeing him.

"Well, may I?" He gestured inward.

"Why not?" Scarlet sighed. "Fenris, back." The wolf took a few steps backwards. The suit entered the apartment, door sliding shut behind him. Fenris gave him a loud bark of warning.

"He's positively terrifying isn't he? But we all know even the most frightful beast is coded not to harm humans."

"Not this one. A close friend overwrote his coding. He's programed to attack and tear a person to shreds on my command, or if I am threatened. He has twenty times the strength of the strongest of humans, even those enhanced for strength. So try not to annoy me."

"Yes." The suit swallowed. "Yes, of course."

"So, first off, how did you find me?"

"I have a very skilled Finder. He found you today and traced you to this address."

That fucking traveling salesman in the bar, Scarlet thought. "Yes, I believe I met him."

"Yes, I believe you did. Anyway, he found you and I have a proposition for you. May I sit?" The suit indicated towards the small couch to his left. Fenris had come back to sit at Scarlet's feet, never taking his eyes off the man.

"First, who the fuck are you?" Scarlet asked with acid.

"Apologies. I should have led with that, I suppose. You may have heard of me… my name is Joseph Souz, although most people call me Joe." He threw up his bio information. It was all there in the bio but Scarlet did know him by name. Dr. Souz was the lead cyber engineer for Walker Global, the largest cybernetics corporation in the industry, and the best. Most of Scarlet's cyber upgrades were Walker; you could not beat their quality. Souz had designed most of the groundbreaking cybernetics to hit the market, but he was also a recluse. He did not allow his image to be shared with the public so no one knew what he looked like or who he really was. That begged the question: why he would show up in person, and why would he come to her?

Scarlet looked at him suspiciously. "And what is your proposition?"

"We at Walker have had a breakthrough many in the industry have been working on for a very long time. You need not know the specifics. We must share it with an affiliate for production to begin as only they have the required technology and equipment. But we cannot just signal it even encrypted as that is too risky. Even the best encrypted signals can be intercepted." Scarlet knew this was true. Christopher had done it all the time for corp espionage jobs. "Therefore we have saved the information on a data cube, also highly encrypted. We would like you to transport it from Walker to our affiliate in secret. I understand you operate on a not-strictly-legal basis and know how to transport hush-hush items without drawing attention to yourself or your employers. I also hear that you are able to handle yourself if things get a bit rough."

"Why come personally? Why not send an envoy?" Scarlet asked.

"More eyes, and ears? No, this can never be known by anyone but corporate heads until the product is ready to be released," Souz explained.

"I don't know, Joe. This all sounds a bit hinky to me."

"The pay is five hundred thousand credits for a

day's work."

Jesus, Scarlet thought, that could raise her up several levels to a place that made this apartment look like a level 50 dive. She could upgrade her entire cyber suite and bio augment her appearance once again. She would need to anyway after a job this big. It was a huge risk but…

"Okay. I'll do it."

"Great," Souz exclaimed and instantly signaled the details of her mission.

***

Scarlet sped towards Walker Global's East Tower in the relatively light traffic of the upper level. She was supposed to meet an engineer at a large open-air terrace jutting off the side of the tower. The air was clean this high up, so she didn't bother with the shield and flew along buffeted by the wind. She followed the route programmed into the heads-up display, and could see the building. Soon enough the terrace appeared. As she approached, she could see a man in a white work suit standing on the edge of the dock on the terrace. The terrace itself was dotted with trees and seating areas. There were water features and sculptures. *These corps know how to live*, she thought.

Scarlet pulled up next to the dock. "The package!" she yelled, her arm outstretched towards the man.

"You must take me with you!" the man shouted back.

"Not part of the deal," she replied. "Now give me the fucking package!"

"Please, I must go with you." The man was afraid, sweating and anxious.

And then Scarlet heard it, alarms going off inside the building. Right arm still extended she pulled a gun out of her left thigh and pointed it at his head. "The fucking package or I blow your fucking head off." Hesitantly he handed her a small steel box. Scarlet holstered her gun back in the thigh compartment of her armor and placed the box on a panel on the bike. Suddenly the box shot down inside of the bike, where it would appear as part of the bike's structure if they were scanned by anyone: her secret stash only her node could open. While she stashed the box. She immediately found out why the man was so nervous.

Heavily armed armored guards began pouring out of the building, firing on them. *What the fuck!* she thought. Either this was so secret even their own security didn't know it or something was seriously fucked up with this job.

"Please, let me go with you," the man pleaded. Scarlet's first instinct was to just take off, but maybe he could explain exactly what the fuck was going on.

"Shit, okay, hop on, damn it!" she shouted and he jumped on the back, arms wrapped around Scarlet's waist.

The bike rocketed off. Scarlet didn't get more than a hundred yards before she felt a heavy impact on her back. The armor absorbed the hit, but it still hurt like hell. She looked back briefly to see the man falling down the levels with a giant hole in his chest. The bike's proximity alert went off and Scarlet's heads-up showed a missile following. It identified as a smart missile that had tagged her: it would follow until impact.

Scarlet brought the bike into a nosedive. The missile would follow but maybe if she got down to the crowed levels, she could shake it or run it into something. She kept dropping until she flew into the middle of heavy traffic, she then leveled out and started evasive maneuvers. She weaved over, under and between vehicles with the missile following adeptly behind, dodging the vehicles with ease. Scarlet dove, inclined, spun around skybridges and through holo ads, all to no avail. The missile stayed right behind her. She spiraled down, dropping dozens of levels, hoping someone would run into it. She would feel bad for the person who hit it but fuck it, she was out of ideas.

Suddenly there was an explosion right behind her and

the bike went spinning out of control. As she tried to right the bike she could see the flashing red and blue lights. As she got control she saw two police vehicles speeding down towards her. They must have shot the missile down.

"You have been tethered. Please dock your vehicle or we will drag your ass to the station. It will not be a comfortable trip."

MIDNIGHT ON THE MIDWAY

By J. L. Aarne.

"They say… They say down here we live in endless night, that's why we worship gods of fire," the man slumped in the chair across from Tick-Tock said in a dull, faraway voice.

His name was Karl and he was a frequent customer, and like most junkies Tick-Tock sold to, he had come to believe that they were friends. Tick-Tock didn't have friends and he wouldn't have had hotheads for friends even if he did. Karl was relaxed now, but an hour earlier he had dived off a ten-story high skybridge onto a car and brought it crashing to the street below. No one had died, but the police were looking for a man fitting Karl's description, so Karl was hiding out at Tick-Tock's place while he came down.

"Gods of fire," Karl repeated. He scratched the back of his head and shifted his eyes to Tick-Tock to make sure he was listening.

Tricky's orange cat Fox was curled up in Tick-Tock's lap and he stroked it while the animal purred. Tricky had gone out with some of her actor friends and wouldn't be home until morning. Karl would be long gone by then, one way or another.

"Do you know his name?" Karl asked.

"Whose name?" Tick-Tock asked.

"The god of fire," Karl said. He scratched harder at his scalp behind his right ear.

Tick-Tock didn't believe in gods and he doubted Karl did either. If Karl had a god, his name was Event Horizon; he prayed by injecting his god into his veins and God answered him by flooding his brain with endorphins and bathing his muscles in adrenalin. Karl's god was a spike of nanobots that turned him into a superhero for a little while.

"No," Tick-Tock said.

Karl sighed. "Me either. They're cruel though, you know?"

"The gods of fire are?"

"Sure, they are, but they keep us warm."

There were people—people a lot different than Karl or Tick-Tock—who still prayed and believed in things like heaven and hell and sin. There would always be people like that. If the world ended tomorrow, the survivors would pull themselves from the ashes and build effigies to their newly born gods. Some people still believed that the world had been created in six days with a few whispered words. That it would be unmade the same way. Tick-Tock wasn't the sort of man who believed such nonsense, but he was the sort of man who would say the words just to see what would happen, even if it might crack the world in two like an egg.

"You think they're still looking for me?" Karl asked.

"Yes," Tick-Tock said. Then, because he wanted Karl to leave, he added, "They would have moved on by now though."

"You think?"

"Yes."

"Maybe you're right."

"Karl, you can't stay here."

Fox got tired of Tick-Tock's lap, hopped down and wandered off toward the kitchen.

"What you mean, I can't?" Karl asked. He sat up straight and looked a bit alarmed. "You said I could, Tick. You said—"

"I said you could wait here until they were gone," Tick-Tock said. "They're gone. You should go home."

It was spoken like a suggestion, but Karl understood it was an order. He stood up nervously, still scratching his head, and started for the door.

"You wouldn't just say that, would you, Tick-Tock?"

"Karl, I like you," Tick-Tock lied. "I don't want the cops to get you, do I? You're one of my best customers. Now, I can't get paid if you're locked up. Thing is, this is my house, but I don't live here alone. If you're still here when my girl gets home, you and me are going to have a problem."

Tick-Tock stood. He was taller than Karl, but Karl was bigger; heavier, more muscular and broader through the shoulders. Karl looked like the dog any sensible person would bet on in a fight, but he took a cautious step in retreat when Tick-Tock got to his feet.

"You're fine, Karl, and much as I enjoy our conversations, it's late and I don't need the cops knocking on my door or Tricky coming home to find you here." Tick-Tock walked by him toward the door, leaving Karl with little choice but to follow. "Bertoldo will walk you out."

Bertoldo had stood quietly since Karl arrived against the wall beside the door. He nodded his pale bald head as Tick-Tock spoke and opened the door for Karl. Bertoldo was bigger than Karl and taller than Tick-Tock, but the most intimidating thing about him was the horns. He had eight of them protruding from his skull like a crown of nails. The surgical implants didn't have any practical use and were cosmetic, but the look was frightening and when Bertoldo narrowed his eyes and nodded toward the door, Karl went without a word.

Tick-Tock was strong enough to pick Karl up and twist him like a wet towel, but he kept Bertoldo around so he wouldn't have to resort to such things. Killing one's regular customers was a poor way to do business.

When they were gone, Tick-Tock went into the kitchen to feed the cat and make himself a coffee. Tricky had left him a note recording on the fridge and he hit a button to play it. Her sultry familiar voice filled the kitchen and he smiled briefly.

"I talked to Todd today. Don't be mad, Tick, he just wants to come home. He's sorry, you know he's sorry. It was an awful thing he did, but it was a long time ago, and Tick-Tock… he's one of us. He said… He said he'll talk to you soon. Do try not to… well, you know. Be good. Don't fight."

Tick-Tock leaned his hip against the counter and sipped his coffee, thinking it wouldn't be much of a fight this time. Todd was beaten, pathetic, and of no use to them anymore. He had outlived his usefulness the moment he stepped off the wall and went over it into the Fringe, taking Tick-Tock and Tricky with him. Given another chance, he would try it again. Tricky was wrong; Todd wasn't one of them anymore, he was a liability. Tick-Tock had been merciful because they had survived and because he understood why Todd did it. He would not be merciful a second time.

He lifted his right hand and stared at it. It looked real enough, the craftsman who had made it did exceptional work. It looked like Tick-Tock's flesh, right down to the warm brown tone of his skin. The surgeons who had installed it, along with the rest, had done excellent work as well. The dexterity of his fingers was superior to any organic human hand, the strength of his arm was such that he could crush a rock in his fist like it was an apricot. But he would never feel with those fingers again. A good portion of his upper body had been replaced with biotech augmentation and it had been necessary because Todd couldn't handle his shit.

Tricky's voice drew Tick-Tock's attention away from examining his fingers in the dull light. "Jason got us a suite at the Sorium. I'm meeting him there, so I'll see you tomorrow. Remember, you're coming to the show tomorrow night. You promised."

Tick-Tock curled his lip in distaste. She was staying the night with her pampered lover. How was he supposed to protect her when she refused to let him? Jason Matsuo was not a safe man to get close to, not for someone like Tricky. They had money, Tick-Tock made sure they always had more than enough money to be comfortable, but Matsuo was 1Akuz0 and married, his father was the corporation's patriarch. Tricky was a dancer and Tick-Tock smuggled drugs into the city from the Fringe; not good company for the spoiled heir of the 1Akuz0 to be associating with, but Tricky didn't care about things like that. She was in love.

Worrying about things like that was Tick-Tock's job.

"Boss?"

Tick-Tock looked up and found Bertoldo standing there, eyeing him with concern. "I'm fine," he said.

"Sure, Boss," Bertoldo said. "I sent the little guy off."

Tick-Tock nodded. "Go on home then. I'll see you tomorrow."

"You sure?"

"I'm sure."

He left and Tick-Tock went back to the living room to sit. He was tired, it had been a long day, and though he didn't like it, he needed to rest. Sleep overtook him almost the moment he relaxed back into his chair.

* * *

He didn't see Tricky until the next evening at the Black Theatre. Tick-Tock was standing on the walkway outside of the Sorium Hotel that morning wearing Tricky's clothes when he came to. She left him with a hangover. It took him until around noon to get rid of, and it put him in a foul mood. He still hadn't shaken it completely by that evening when he made his way toward the outer edge of Arc City to the Black Theater where Tricky performed.

Some of it was his irritation with Tricky's recklessness, but she had always been reckless. A free spirit she might have been called in earlier days. Or a fool. He loved her, but she never had been the type to consider the consequences of her actions. "That's why I have you, Tick," she'd say. It was true, but he sometimes found himself wishing she wouldn't make his job so damn hard.

The Black Theater was a strange building. It was only five stories high and the architecture resembled that of an 18th century Parisian theater rather than a building one would expect to see squatting amid the sleek corporate towers and housing units of Arc. The outside of the building was entirely black, even the glass was tinted and could only be looked through from the inside.

Tick-Tock fell in beside a group of young people also going to the theater as he approached the fifteen-foot-high black steel gate entrance and overheard them laughing and talking about it. They were upper middle-class kids, thrilled to be slumming it. They were nervous to be so close to the Fringe and excited by the adventure of doing something their parents would so thoroughly disapprove of.

"I heard they have a cloned Tiger. A real one," a boy said. He had messy black hair and he had dressed down for the occasion but still looked like a rich kid wearing a poor man's costume.

"They do not," a girl to the boy's right said. "How could they have a tiger? There are laws. It's not—"

Tick-Tock passed them and walked through the archway under the watchful eyes of robotic gargoyles standing guard at the entrance. A short white man named Marshal with a leathery face and a holographic tattoo over one eye scanning customers and taking payment for the show waved him through. He also stamped the back of customers' hands as they paid and the boy who had been talking about the tiger held his up to look at it. The stamp was a useless bit of kitsch, but the Black Theater was a kitschy sort of place.

"They do not have a tiger, Leore."

The young couple were right behind him and Tick-Tock smiled faintly to himself. Jon, the old man who owned the theater, had once had a tiger, but it had been an unexceptional clone. Cloned from already cloned genetic material degraded by many generations of cloning, the animal had been half the size of the stunning extinct beasts from which it had been descended. Tigger, Jon had called it, after some 20th century cartoon character.

Tigger had died the previous winter. Cancer, Tricky had told him.

Inside, Tick-Tock took the stairs down to the ground level and walked onto a wide round floor. There were hundreds of people already milling about, talking and laughing, waiting for the show. Above, there were five levels of galleries filled with people, some of them laughing, some leaning dangerously out over the railing. In the past, such a structure would have been described as having a soaring vaulted ceiling, but they now lived in a time when five stories was a very short building indeed and you could stand in the atrium of most buildings and the ceiling was a thousand feet above your head. By comparison, the Black Theater was almost cozy and the atmosphere somewhat claustrophobic.

Backstage, it was a different world. There were half naked men painting their faces and lining their eyes in front of mirrors. Topless candy dancers in red and white striped tutus adjusted their fluffy cotton candy pink wigs and iced their nipples. Discarded costumes were tossed over chairs or left on the floor to be walked on.

A girl named Ella who did a bizarre living-puppet act nearly ran into Tick-Tock in her rush to finish setting up. She wore a thin shirt backstage, but it would come off when it was her cue. Her skin was pierced with hundreds of tiny rings through which small cables were hooked so that gradually she could be lifted into the air. It was a shocking performance, but the crowd loved her.

She stepped back and smiled at him. "Sorry, honey. Things to do, you know?" she said and hurried off.

Tick-Tock was a familiar face and none of the actors paid him any attention as he walked among them. They were too busy putting the finishing touches on their makeup and making sure they knew their lines. The Black Theater wasn't known for dramatic plays, they didn't do Shakespeare, but there was a certain level of drama and acting to the strange vaudeville freakshow nonetheless.

There was a crack of light between the wall and the curtain, and Tick-Tock went to stand where he could look through it. Out on the floor, girls went through the crowd offering drinks and sweets. The candy was laced with more than just sugar, he knew because old Jon was one of his best, most reliable customers. Event Horizon—or Fire Hat as some had started calling it—wasn't the kind of drug that could be taken orally, but it wasn't the only thing Tick-Tock sold. The drugs heightened the experience, but the show itself was quite the experience without them in his opinion.

A young girl named Vel with a monkey on her shoulder approached him and Tick-Tock turned his head to look at her just as the monkey reached out with something in its hand. Tick-Tock took it. It was a round, purple piece of candy wrapped in plastic.

"Thanks," Tick-Tock said.

"Sure. You looked like you could use it," Vel said.

"You know… to mellow out."

Tick-Tock smiled to himself as she walked away. Tick-Tock was the most mellow person he knew. He unwrapped the candy and popped it in his mouth. It was grape with an odd fizziness that denoted the presence of a drug called Bubb-LE. Not what the candy for patrons at the Black Theater was usually laced with. It had no psychotropic effects, it was something kept on hand for the actors and dancers to take the edge off.

The show opened at the Black Theater four nights a week. The theater attracted the strange, the unusual and the outcasts because that was what it promised. Arc City had many such people, so the acts weren't always the same. The living puppet act was one of the theater's great attractions, but Ella always needed at least a day to recover. There was a magician who called himself Mordechai who only worked on Saturdays. Tricky worked the theater three nights a week and she only did that because she loved it. It certainly wasn't for the money. She liked the attention and she loved how it felt to move, to be desired because she was beautiful and strange. It was what had first drawn her to Jason, Tick-Tock was sure. He looked so much like a fairy tale prince, though he was a dragon underneath. Her favorite stories as a kid had always been the ones where the princesses saved themselves and loved fierce beasts, not weak princes.

Part of the problem was she thought it was romantic, knowing her lover was a monster, yet loving him anyway.

As the curtains went up and the show started, Tick-Tock watched from the sidelines and his eyes shifted away from the topless dancers tossing candy to the crowd. His gaze fell on Jason Matsuo in the second row from the front. He was there with his wife and Tick-Tock's jaw clenched in anger.

"The first time I saw her, I thought, 'she looks like sunlight,'" Tricky told him once, it had been long ago when her relationship with the woman's husband was new.

"I don't even know why I thought it or what it meant. Isn't that weird, Tick?"

The candy dancers left the stage and the lights that had been diming went out completely, casting everything into absolute darkness. At first, only a pinprick of light appeared in the center of the stage, bright and blue. Slowly, the light broadened and in the center of it was Tricky, kneeling on the floor, her body folded, arms outstretched. Veins of blue light twisted and scattered along the dark skin of her right arm and when she lifted her head and turned her face to the audience, the bright veins ran up her neck, over the right side of her face and that eye, the artificial one, glowed until it lit up the whole theater like foxfire.

I did that, Todd whispered in Tick-Tock's mind and he flinched. The voice was an echo, something disembodied and far away, but it caught him by surprise. *Did I do that?*

On stage, Tricky rose from the floor in a sinuous curve of the body that would have been impossible for a person without cybernetic enhancements like hers to achieve. After Todd tried to kill her, Tick-Tock had paid to replace her right arm, the right half of her skull, one eye, her spinal column, and the first seven ribs on the right side as well as the skin, which perfectly matched and was indistinguishable from the natural dark brown tone of her body. The only noticeable difference in daylight was the cybernetic blue eye that didn't match the brown left one, but in the dark under certain light her skin lit up with veins like tiny fiberoptic cables, which as she danced created tracers in the dark. The left side of her body was covered in UV tattoos that gave off a duller glow, but as she moved, her body became a sensual, mesmerizing lightshow.

They called her the Lady of Serpents for the way she moved, her androgynous body swaying smoothly, twisting impossibly. Her hair of tiny braids fell loose nearly to her waist, Medusa-like. Her full, smiling mouth was coated in pearlescent gloss and her teeth flashed whiter than white in the dark. She wore nothing except for lace stockings, platform stiletto heels and a stomacher of glowing green and blue stones that did nothing at all to hide her nakedness, her genitals, her every curve and muscle, natural or artificial, from her adoring audience. Tricky looked otherworldly and exotic, like a goddess of some wild, undiscovered place. When she was in her element like this, every man and woman looking wanted her and she knew it. Tick-Tock pulled his attention away from her to look out at the faces of those gathered below the stage. Their eyes and teeth glowed grotesquely in the blacklight. It felt like the crowd of a thousand was collectively holding its breath.

Tricky reached into a basket and pulled out a python. The big snake also glowed, though it was green rather than blue. There were gasps as she leaned out toward the people closest to the stage with the snake and Tricky's teeth glowed as she grinned. The python wound around her arm, over her hand, and floated off the tips of her fingers, where it slithered six feet off the ground through the crowd. The glow of it illuminated their upturned, amazed faces as it passed.

Abruptly, all the lights went out and a murmur arose in the audience, punctuated by a few nervous little cries of alarm.

When the lights slowly came up, Tricky was gone. Silk streamers descended from the ceiling and two people, a man and woman with light olive skin and two cybernetic arms on each side below the arms they had been born with took the spotlight.

Tricky had disappeared when the lights went out and reappeared when they came back on standing with Tick-Tock. "We need to talk, don't we?" she asked.

He sighed. "Go get your things."

"Tick—"

"We'll talk," he said. "Not here, at home."

"You saw Jason, didn't you?" Tricky asked.

"I saw him," Tick-Tock said. "And I saw his wife."

"He doesn't love her," Tricky said.

"Tricky."

She heard the warning in his voice but chose to ignore it. "She doesn't love him either, it—"

"Go get dressed. We'll talk at home."

Tricky wanted to argue about it then and there, but she knew what it meant when he sounded like that, so she went to her dressing room instead.

***

They were both quiet on the way home. Tricky was quiet because she thought Tick-Tock was mad. He let her think it.

The silence lasted until they were in the elevator. "I love him, Tick."

Tick-Tock rolled his eyes. "So what?" he said.

"So, I *love* him," she said more forcefully.

And that was all that should matter. She didn't say it, but she didn't need to. Tick-Tock knew her better than anyone ever had or could. If Tricky had a fatal weakness, it was that she wanted desperately to be loved. She always had. It didn't matter that it never worked out. It made no difference that she always tried to love the wrong people. There was irony here somewhere; a voracious huger to be loved, an outdated romantic idea of what that meant, and an inclination for entangling herself with worthless, unlovable garbage like Jason Matsuo.

"That doesn't matter," Tick-Tock said.

"It matters," Tricky muttered.

"It does not matter. He doesn't love you, so it does not matter," Tick-Tock said.

"You don't—"

"Yes, I do. I do know that," he interrupted.

The elevator numbers flicked by above the door: 78, 79, 80...

"You're not stupid. You know better, don't you?"

"Don't talk to me like I'm a child, Tick. I'm not a little girl."

Tick-Tock sighed. That had not been his intention, as he was sure she was aware, but she didn't want to think about it. She did know better, and she didn't like what she knew.

"He was angry this morning," she said, soft and reluctantly. "He... Mariko must have said something to him, and he was so angry, I left. But he said... He said he'd never let me go."

Tick-Tock didn't bother to ask if Jason had hit her. The man had it in him, Tick-Tock didn't doubt that, but there was no need. If he had hit her, Tick-Tock would have awakened inside the hotel room, not out on the street.

Outside the windows, the air grew clearer as the numbers flashed on: 99, 100, 101...

"He's bad for you and something is going to happen if you don't cut him loose," Tick-Tock said.

"But I love him," she whispered.

She started to silently cry and Tick-Tock lifted a hand to wipe away the tears. "What does he always say to you?"

"W-what?"

"That thing he says that drives you crazy."

She swallowed and licked her lips. "He always... When he leaves first, he always says he has to get back to the real world."

"And you hate it."

"I *am* real. It's like... like I'm not real to him. Yes, I hate it."

Tick-Tock tried not to gloat, but he smiled just a little anyway. "Yeah."

"You don't care about Mariko Matsuo," Tricky said. "Don't pretend. I know you don't give a damn about her."

"I don't," he agreed. "I care that her husband is a powerful man used to having what he wants—*everything* he wants—and you threaten that because of her. Most people like him have only a few ways of dealing with threats like that, and none of them end with you being alive, free and happy."

Tricky couldn't argue with that and she didn't try. She fell into thoughtful, brooding silence for a while.

The floor number lit up at 120, the elevator stopped, and the doors swept open.

"We should really talk about Todd," Tricky said as they left the elevator.

Two of Tick-Tock's men were waiting outside their door. One of them was Bertoldo and he stepped away from the wall and started toward Tick-Tock as they approached. He looked worried and right away that got Tick-Tock's attention. Bertoldo didn't get rattled easily.

"Did you hear me? Tick, we—"

Tick-Tock cut her off, "Not now, something's wrong."

Bertoldo's breath puffed as he came to a stop in front of Tick-Tock. He was a big man and intimidating to have around, but he wasn't particularly athletic. The short jog from one end of the long hall to the other winded him.

Looking at him, Tick-Tock decided to make Bertoldo go see the doctor for a checkup soon. "What is it?" he asked.

"Boss… we tried to get you on the comm…" Bertoldo huffed. "We tried, but…"

Tick-Tock didn't have a communication implant, he still used the old wristband. It was low-tech, but it was more secure. He left his comm device at home when he went out with Tricky most of the time so he wouldn't be bothered.

He gestured impatiently for Bertoldo to get to the point. "What is it?"

"It's that junkie, Karl."

Without waiting for further explanation, Tick-Tock went around Bertoldo and started down the hall. The bigger man hurried to catch up.

"He's lost it, Boss. Gone full-on cysyc," Bertoldo panted. "We tried to stop him… but he… he's got the eyes and that smile, don't nobody want to get near him."

The other man by the door who hadn't moved from his at ease position against the wall nodded to Tick-Tock. His name was Mike and he had been raised by a single mother high up in the matriarchal Walker Global Corporation and, from what Tick-Tock understood, she had been a stern woman who preferred her children to be silent. He wasn't much of a talker. Tick-Tock respected that and had come to expect that what Mike said was to the point and true.

"What the hell's going on in there, Mike?"

"I could only guess, sir," Mike said. "I would guess, from the noise inside, he's searching for something."

"Drugs," Tick-Tock said.

Mike nodded. "I suspect so."

Tick-Tock glanced between the two men, saw that they were afraid, and sighed. He left them in the hall and went inside.

Tick-Tock and Tricky weren't as wealthy as some of the higher ranking people who squabbled their way to the top of the corporate houses, but they were doing okay. They lived at the top of a great sky tower, they ate real food, they breathed clean air, there was a garden atrium in the center of their house where they had real plants and a woman came in three days a week to clean the residence. They were comfortable. Tick-Tock was a businessman and he was very good at what he did. He was even better at making sure no one knew that he did it.

Guys like Karl were a calculated risk that people in Tick-Tock's business had to take. However, once they became a true threat, the potential cost outweighed that risk. Karl was now a liability.

"Karl," Tick-Tock called.

He reached over on the wall inside the door and flipped open the casing on the control pad for the home computer. It had been acting up and he kept meaning to have someone come in and fix it, but in the meantime, the security settings had been turned down low so that it wouldn't mistake one of his men, Tricky or Tick-Tock himself for an intruder. He turned it back up and closed the casing. Hopefully he wasn't about to have his head blown off by his own home security system.

"Karl? You here?"

He could see evidence of Karl's search for the drugs he wanted. In the kitchen, cupboard doors stood open, drawers were pulled out and dumped on the floor, papers that had been stacked neatly on the table in the living room were strewn everywhere, one of the plush easy chairs by the coffee table had been overturned, the upholstery of it and the other chair cut open. Tick-Tock frowned as he made his way from room to room, but he didn't become truly angry until he came upon one of Tricky's camisoles dangling by a lace strap from the doorknob of their bedroom.

"Karl?!" he shouted. He tried not to let the anger seep into his voice, but he heard it there anyway. "Come on, Karl. You hiding from me? What for? You want something, man, you gotta come out and ask me for it. I can't read your mind, my friend."

The door to the adjacent bathroom opened and slammed into the wall. The sight of Karl took Tick-Tock slightly aback. He had expected to find the man in the earliest stages of crazed withdrawal. Instead, Karl appeared to be on the verge of a rampage. His eyes were wide and crazed, his face was split wide-open in a hideous grin and he was vibrating in place with suppressed energy. No wonder his men had stood outside and not tried to stop him. Karl was completely psychotic and would have killed them both like they were nothing.

"Hey there Tick," Karl said.

Tick-Tock watched his mouth open around the words, his lips never drooping from his mad, stretched

Cheshire Cat grin. He calculated the distance between himself and Karl, and wondered if he could take him if he had to. It was possible, he decided.

"What can I do for you, Karl?"

"I need more juice, Tick. Juice, you know? Gotta have it," Karl said. He started walking toward him and when Tick-Tock stood his ground he laughed. "I know you got it. Got it here somewhere, don't you? Hid it, I bet. You're gonna give it to me though or I'm gonna rip your arms off just like they was the wings on a fly."

Tick-Tock spread his arms, showing Karl his empty hands. "Sorry, Karl. I'm all out."

"LIAR!"

"Computer, activate maximum security protocols," Tick-Tock said calmly.

There was a soft musical sound overhead like the chime of a bell before a compartment in the ceiling opened and a large, sleek gun lowered and aimed at Karl. A tiny red dot appeared in the center of Karl's chest. "Intruder, please raise your hands above your head," ordered a soft, serene recorded voice.

Karl laughed again. "What the fuck is that supposed to be?"

Tricky had programmed the home computer's settings to a voice she said reminded her of some actress from the 21st century she liked named Sigourney Weaver. Either the voice perplexed him, or Karl had never had a high energy laser rifle pointed at him before.

"Do what she says," Tick-Tock said. "Walk out of here now or I'm going to tell her to blow a nice fist-sized hole through your heart."

Karl laughed again and it was really starting to get on Tick-Tock's nerves.

"You have ten seconds to comply," Sigourney Weaver said.

"I need more, Tick," Karl said, ignoring the computer as it started to count. "I gotta have it. I know you got some around here somewhere. I *know* you do. You better give it to me."

Karl paid no attention to the computer and started toward him. He was fast but Tick-Tock was just a tiny bit faster. He turned and backed up, moving at the last moment out of Karl's path so that Karl's momentum carried him forward into the wall. Karl caught himself against the wall, bounced back and launched himself again at Tick-Tock.

Tick-Tock turned, kicked him and Karl slammed into the armoire. Tick-Tock winced at the crash of Karl's hopped-up body against the antique wood. It had been a twenty-fifth birthday present for Tricky and it sounded like something had cracked when Karl hit it.

The computer was counting down "five…four…"

"Countdown override," Tick-Tock said as Karl screamed wordlessly at him and charged again. "Fire."

The laser rifle fired, the bright white bolt didn't miss, but Karl dodged, and it cut across his back. He didn't even flinch. The computer should have been able to predict Karl's movements and anticipate his actions, but it was too slow. It fired and missed again, the shots going over his back and punching holes in the bedroom wall.

Tick-Tock cursed and had time to raise his hand before Karl grabbed him. His hand was strong and unyielding as it closed around Tick-Tock's throat, but it was flesh and bone because Karl spent all his money on his drug habit. Tick-Tock raised his own hand, closed his fingers around Karl's throat and squeezed. Karl choked and his wide, mad eyes registered shock and fear for an instant before a pulse of energy from the palm of Tick-Tock's hand disintegrated the tissue of his throat and the bones of his spinal cord, effectively severing his head from his body.

Disgusted, Tick-Tock dropped Karl's body on the floor, inspected his hands, straightened his coat and walked back through the house to let Mike and Bertoldo in.

The two men stared at the body in dumbfounded silence. They knew there was more to their boss than most people suspected or than Tick-Tock ever let on, but they rarely witnessed it themselves. He was a scary guy, they all knew it, but he wasn't big, he was quiet, and there was Tricky. Some of them thought she made him weak, though none of them ever said so within his hearing.

"Ah… so, what happened?" Bertoldo asked.

"I took care of it," Tick-Tock said. "Clean this up, get rid of the body."

"I'll do it, sir," Mike said. "I'll just… call some of the guys."

"Call that cleaner, Marcus. I like him," Tick-Tock said. "And get someone to fix that stupid fucking computer."

"Sure, whatever you want," Bertoldo said. The two men exchanged nervous glances. "Are you—?"

"We're going out tonight, you can take care of it while we're out. Now, I'm taking a shower, I don't want to be bothered," Tick-Tock said, gesturing at Karl's body. "Get that out of here."

They hurried to pick up the body and carry it out of the bedroom.

"You want anything else, sir?" Mike asked.

"No." Tick-Tock started to close the door, then opened it again and looked out. "Make sure the voice is the same."

"The voice?"

"The computer. The AI. It has the voice of some actress, tell them to leave it."

They looked confused, but they both nodded.

Tick-Tock closed the door and went to clean up.

"Are you okay?" Tricky asked him as he stripped to get into the shower.

"I'm fine," he said.

She took his word for it. "So, where are we going?"

* * *

They saw a play at one of the sky theaters. The actors walked across a floating stage and played out a story of tragic, one-sided unrequited love. At the end, the man who adored the beautiful princess who never looked at him the way he wanted her to died of a broken heart, vomiting up flowers that choked the life out of him.

Tricky wore one of her favorite gowns, a gold and white thing made to look like the costume of a Victorian lady. She coiled her hair atop her head and lined her eyes with liquid gold, and she wept when the doomed lover died and his beloved realized the source of his illness too late.

"Did you pick that play on purpose?" she asked Tick-Tock when they were in the car going home.

"I thought you would like it," he said.

"I *mean*… You know what I mean," she said. "Were you trying to teach me a lesson, Tick?"

He sighed. "No."

"No," she said thoughtfully. "You're not like that."

"It doesn't mean anything, I just thought you would enjoy it," he said.

"It's a coincidence then?" she said. "Me and Jason, those two—"

"I could have taken you to a different theater, we could have seen *Romeo and Juliet*," he said. "You might have found some meaning in that, too. It's just a play."

"I'm not going to see him anymore," she said.

"What?"

"You heard me. You win. I won't see Jason anymore."

"It's not about me winning."

"It kind of is. Maybe just a little, but it is."

***

A programmer came by the next day to work on the

glitchy home computer. She declared the entire thing a disaster and in need of an upgrade after working on it for an hour, and left with a promise to return when she had a new one ready to install. Until then, Tick-Tock made sure to have his best people watching the place because the only security there was stopped at the elevator.

He returned home after a long day to find Mrs. Matsuo waiting outside the door with the two men assigned to guard the place. They had set up a hover table and were playing cards while they waited for their shift to end. Mariko Matsuo sat in a third chair watching them play. She looked uncomfortable, but her nerves were not because of the men, which became clear when she saw Tick-Tock and jumped to her feet.

She bowed and he acknowledged her with a bow of his own out of courtesy.

"I'm sorry to disturb you at your home. I need to speak with you if I may," she said.

Tick-Tock studied her and immediately knew that she had mistaken him for Tricky. He didn't hold it against her; it was an easy enough mistake to make. He also didn't correct her assumption, but decided to play along.

"There is no need to apologize," he said. "Come inside."

She followed him into the house and Tick-Tock ordered tea from the kitchen. He had to make the order manually from the menu without the home computer, but it took only a minute. They sat and when the tea arrived, Mariko Matsuo thanked him. She picked up the cup and saucer and held it. Everything was done without making eye contact.

"Has something happened?" Tick-Tock asked when she still didn't speak.

"Yes, something has happened," she said. One of her hands went to her stomach and she finally raised her head to look him in the eye, though only briefly. "I would not have come here, I do not mean to shame you or…"

"Then why did you come?" he asked.

"To ask you… To beg you, if I must," she said. Her voice grew so soft it was almost a whisper and broke like she might start to cry. She swallowed and drew herself up. "You know that we are married?"

"You and Jason. Yes, I know."

"It's ceremonial—traditional—but our families would not look kindly upon your relationship with my husband. It could be ignored before, but…"

"You're pregnant," Tick-Tock guessed.

She nodded. "It would shame our families and shame my husband if your relationship became public."

It would bring shame to her as well, but that went without saying.

"And I'm guessing your husband can't allow that to happen, can he?" Tick-Tock asked. "He's a proud man."

"It is a little thing, no one much cares about it anymore, but there would be whispers.

"And whispers might be enough."

"Yes."

Monogamy wasn't expected in marriage anymore, but discretion was, and Jason Matsuo liked to flaunt it by taking his wife to the Black Theater to watch his girlfriend dance naked before the lowly masses.

Tick-Tock sat back and sipped his tea. Then he said, "All right."

She looked up at him, surprised. "All right?"

"Yeah. It's over," he said. "I won't see him anymore."

"Just like that?" she asked doubtfully.

"Just like that," Tick-Tock said, and he smiled.

Jason Matsuo was dangerous to them. Todd was dangerous. If Tick-Tock could completely get rid of one of them, it would make dealing with the other that much easier. Tricky had sworn to him that she was finished with Jason, so Tick-Tock felt no compunction whatsoever about making it official.

"Thank you," Mariko Matsuo said. "I know it's very

antiquated."

"It's tradition, I understand," Tick-Tock said.

He did, too. The governing families got a lot of their power from their traditions. It was how they stayed in power. The woman sitting across from him had no idea who he was, or who Tricky really was for that matter. It would not occur to her that, as an outlier, Tick-Tock had power, too. Mrs. Matsuo embodied the ideal meek, submissive wife making a request, but she was anything but. Tricky was not and had never been her rival as far as she was concerned; her visit was a courtesy made to avoid violence, but she was giving an order. It didn't sound like an order and it hadn't been presented as one, but it was an order just the same. Luckily for her and her husband's family, Tick-Tock saw it to be in his and Tricky's best interests to follow that order. He had too much to lose to risk going to war with the 1Akuz0 over something so trivial.

"It's over, I promise," he said.

She set her tea cup down on the table carefully, the tea untouched. "Thank you," she said.

Tick-Tock stood as she did, but she left quickly without giving him a chance to walk her to the door.

When she was gone, he sat back down and finished his tea, staring thoughtfully out the window that ran the length of the northern wall of the house. The VR screen was off, so it looked down on the city in real time. He could see the 1Akuz0 tower in the distance piercing the sky through the clouds. He had never been inside it, he would not have been welcome there. Some of its citizens were his customers, but they would not want anyone to know that. There had never been any reason for him to go there and, unless Tricky had lied to him, which she never did, she had never been there either.

He wondered if Jason was there now.

***

When he told Tricky about Mariko Matsuo's visit and what he had done, she cried. She shouted at him for a little while, to the alarm of the men stationed outside their door, but it didn't last long. She had meant it when she promised to break things off with Jason, so he was already half gone when Tick-Tock put an end to it. She was just mad that it had been Tick-Tock who ended it.

She cried for a long time and he sat with her in a chair pulled up close to the window and let her cry. After a while, with the tears drying on her face, she asked him about Todd again. Again, he told her no and she cried for a little bit longer.

After the jump off the wall that everyone insisted on calling an accident, there had been a doctor. Officially, "the accident" was deemed an attempted suicide, so a doctor was assigned to them. By then, Tick-Tock had gotten rid of Todd. He couldn't kill him like he would have if anyone else had done what Todd did, but he could make sure that Todd would never be able hurt them again. The doctor was good for Tricky for a while. She helped her a lot. Then she started trying to bring Todd back into their lives. She believed that Todd was important and that he was supposed to be there.

That had been the end of their visits with the well-meaning doctor.

They had each other, Tricky said, they didn't need anyone else. Tick-Tock had silently agreed and then he had done his best to help her move on. It hadn't been easy, and it had taken a long time, but they were there now. They had moved on from Todd.

Tricky hadn't cried so hard since Todd; like her heart was broken. Tears and snot and hiccups that made her shake. He hoped it meant that she was letting Jason go the way she had let Todd go years before.

"Tell me a story, Tick," she said, wiping at her wet face. "Tell me a story about the night lands."

The night lands were what they called the dead world

beyond the wall. The vast, uncivilized territory on the other side of the Fringe that comprised almost everything between Arc and the next city. The night lands were full of abandoned places, homes and vast ground level cities that had fallen to ruin and dust. They were overgrown with trees and moss and rot until they became habitat for animals again like they had been thousands of years ago. Tricky's mother had called them the night lands and they still thought of them that way long after she was gone.

"Tell me a story," she said again.

"All right," he said. He watched the bright lights of the city below and the holographic advertisements cast on the outside of the buildings as he began to tell her a story about a faraway place that had never seen such things or needed them. "Everyone knew no one lived in the night lands, but that wasn't quite true…"

* * *

It took a few days, but then Jason Matsuo's men came for her. They came at night while Tricky was out.

Tick-Tock had finished his business for the day. He ordered a drink from the kitchen and the newly upgraded home computer had it made and delivered to him while he lay down to read in bed.

They were quiet. He didn't hear them until they were inside the house. Before he heard them, he was alerted to their presence when the cat ran into the bedroom and shot beneath the bed to hide. Tick-Tock put his book aside and went to the door to listen. They were in the living room, it sounded like more than one man but he couldn't be sure.

The outer wall was set to window mode and looked out on the night sky, but Tick-Tock touched it, selected manual control so he wouldn't have to speak and pulled up the security cameras. He counted two men and saw that one had opened the control center of the home computer to disable it before the cameras went black.

Tick-Tock stood with his back against the wall to the right of the bedroom door and waited, listening to their progress through the house. They were good; quiet, careful, and undoubtedly packing some serious 1Akuz0 biotech. Tick-Tock stood beside the door until he heard them draw close, then he moved and stepped around Tricky's armoire so that they wouldn't see him when they entered the room.

They went straight for the bed when they came into the room and Tick-Tock moved in the second they were caught off guard by its emptiness. He rushed them and shot the smaller man with the pulse weapon in his right hand. It wasn't a killing shot and the man tried to get up and come after him even with a fist-sized hole through his left shoulder. Tick-Tock had to dodge a shot from the other man's weapon before he could shoot him again. The second shot was to the face and he didn't get up that time.

"You're going to pay for that," the bigger man said. Both men were dressed head to toe in black, including a fukumen, so all that Tick-Tock could see were his eyes. Both eyes were bright cyber blue.

Tick-Tock didn't wait to hear how he was going to pay, he turned his right hand toward him and fired again. He didn't miss, but one moment the assassin was there, the next he wasn't. He moved, spun and knocked Tick-Tock to the floor. Even as Tick-Tock was getting up, his mind was racing to find an escape. The assassin was faster than he was. More of his body was cybernetic, some of it higher grade tech than Tick-Tock's. He was bigger and stronger and faster. The pulse weapon in Tick-Tock's hand took about a minute to recharge after a couple shots and he wasn't going to survive a minute unarmed with the assassin, so he ran.

The assassin had a weapon implant in his arm and fired as he followed him through the house. Tick-Tock felt the energy heat of each shot that got close and expected to die even as he was rushing for the door. Light flashed all around him as the laser weapon fired. Plaster, glass, bits of metal and sparks flew everywhere and rained down on Tick-Tock's back as he tried to stay low and ran.

The door was open and he flew through it a moment before a bolt crashed into the wall beside it, cut a hole through the doorframe and blasted into the outer corridor. Bertoldo's body lay across the threshold and Tick-Tock had only seconds to duck behind it before another shot put a hole in the wall where his head had been.

Cursing, the assassin jumped over the sofa, fell against the glass wall of the atrium and came after him. Tick-Tock had only seconds and didn't waste them. Bertoldo had never had weapon implants, so he always carried at least one sidearm. Tick-Tock stayed low, hidden behind Bertoldo's body and felt inside his jacket. The assassin's footsteps made the floor shake. Tick-Tock's pulse was heavy, tickling his throat. Bertoldo and the other dead guard—a new guy whose name he hadn't committed to memory yet—had bled a lot. Their blood was cold and it seeped through his clothes and filled his mouth and nose with pennies on every breath.

He couldn't find the gun.

"I'm sorry. We might be about to die," he whispered to Tricky, his hand moving over Bertoldo's sides, searching.

"No, Tick, this isn't how we die," she said. She sounded so calm, so sure. "Tick, he's laying on it."

She was right. His hand found the butt of the pistol on the floor, the gun mostly hidden beneath Bertoldo's bulk. He could hear the assassin's heavy breathing as he reached the door. The man hesitated at the door and didn't see Tick-Tock right away. It was only a second. The time it takes a hummingbird to flap its wings a single time.

It was enough. Tick-Tock yanked the gun from beneath the body, brought it up and fired. The end of the barrel was less than a foot from the assassin's face and the blast disintegrated the top of his head. Blood, flesh, brain matter and bone scorched to ashes as the laser blew through him. The body flew back into the house as the ashes fell to the floor and then there was silence.

It was a silence heavy with anticipation and Tick-Tock waited, holding his breath, his pulse like drumbeats in his ears. Nothing happened. No one else appeared.

He let the breath out and stood.

"Now what?" Tricky asked.

"Now we call your boyfriend," he said.

"What? Why?"

"Makes no difference I killed these two. If I don't stop it at the source, more will come."

She didn't say anything for a while. Then she said, "Oh," and that was all. She understood and it made her sad, but she wasn't surprised. "Do you want me to make the call?"

He smiled and flicked the safety button on the gun as he walked back into the house. "You don't have to."

"Tick, I really wish people would stop trying to kill us in our own house," she said.

"Me, too," he said.

Tick-Tock retrieved his comm wristband from the coffee table in the living room where he'd left it and turned it on. "Call Jason Matsuo."

"Calling Jason Matsuo," a small, tinny voice replied, followed by the soft purr of the notification.

"You're going to pretend to be me?" Tricky asked.

"Of course."

"Are you sure you can be me?"

"I only have to be you for a minute."

"Tick."

"I'm sure I can be you. Who knows you better?"

He had her there. She fell silent as Jason answered his comm.

He sounded sleepy. He had sent men to kill Tricky, then the arrogant asshole had gone to bed.

"Tricky?" Jason asked, surprised.

Tick-Tock changed his voice, made it a little higher than normal, altered the cadence to match Tricky's speech, gasped a little breathlessly to sound the way Tricky might sound in Jason's imagination if someone was trying to kill her. "Jason! Jason, someone's here!"

"What?" He sounded more alert. "Tricky? Baby, what's happening?!"

"Jason, there's someone in the house," Tick-Tock said in a frightened whisper. "They did something to the computer, I can't get security to answer. You have to help me."

"Hide somewhere, honey, I'll be right there," he said. "Just hide. It'll take me a few minutes. Can you hide where they won't find you for a few minutes?"

"I think so," Tick-Tock said. "Hurry."

He disconnected the call, tossed the comm device back on the table and muttered, "Moron."

Jason had been raised with privilege and wealth, everything taken care of for him, obstacles removed from his path almost before they were noticed, and consequentially, he had never needed to develop an instinct for survival. He ordered someone dead, he expected them to die and didn't think about it again. If he had been clever, he would have asked more questions. He would have wondered why Tricky didn't use the same communication device she was calling him on to alert the building's security on the main floor. He would have asked why she hadn't called the police. Never mind that his family owned the police, they were the police.

"Why does he want to kill me, Tick?" Tricky asked.

"I don't know. Maybe he found out that his wife visited you. He doesn't know why, she wouldn't have talked to him about it, but..." But Tricky was an unknown threat now. Not a threat to Jason's life, but potentially a threat to his pride. "It doesn't really matter why. When he gets here, I'll take care of it."

She sighed. "I know."

* * *

Later, after Tick-Tock cut Jason's throat, but before he called his men to come clean it all up, they sat together by the window again. It was the middle of the night and they were high enough up and far enough away from the city center that tiny, vague sparks of stars could be seen in the distance. Tricky had once memorized all the constellations. She still remembered some of them.

"I think that's Orion," she told Tick-Tock. "See the belt? It's those three stars. They're brighter, that's why you can still see it even with all the lights."

Tick-Tock looked where she pointed. He could just make out the three little specks of light.

They sat quietly for a minute. There was something on her mind and he let her work it out. Finally, she asked, "Why can't we ever keep anything we love, Tick?"

Jason's body lay on the floor a few feet away. The next day he would be found somewhere across the city, somewhere Jason Matsuo might go if he was looking for a good time. He was known to be rebellious, to party, take risks and frequent places someone of his social status should have given a wide berth. He would be dumped there, in an alleyway or on a street corner, his throat cut with a crude metal blade, and the end of his story would tell itself.

Tick-Tock wanted to believe that Tricky would be more careful with her heart next time, but he doubted it.

"*I* love you," he said.

He gazed into the glass at their reflection in it like a mirror against the dark sky. He saw her looking back, one brown eye, one blue, and she saw him, one brown eye and one blue. The same eyes, two souls, and somewhere buried down deep, there was Todd, though Tick-Tock imagined his view was like that of a trapped creature at the bottom of a dark, forgotten well.

Tricky smiled. "I know you do," she said. "You're

right. We have each other. We don't need anyone else, do we? Not really."

BROADCAST 2220

By Davene Le Grange.

I don't always get why people start with, 'my name is.' Like you care whether I'm Suzy, twenty-two, from Arc-Namania Tower or Borkan, thirty-five, from Arc-Zokul. What difference does it make to you? Well, in my story, how people refer to me does matter.

I go by Sandy, born Astari Tekeryi.

The last part, my real name, is a secret. I'm twenty-five years old, marking eight years since I ran away from my Tekeryi-family name and our quadrillion-dollar industry. It's not that I hated my parents and grandparents, but I didn't fit in or agree with how they kept sending the poor, also known as marlers, to Mars. The promises of a new home and future were lies, but who says no to the opportunity and winning lottery ticket of escaping their hell?

Even I would sacrifice my coffin-box studio for the comfort of my childhood room above the smog-trapping skyscrapers to breathe clean, filtered air from Earth's stratosphere. Tower rings around a space elevator; the arcology was breathtaking, but given the rare choice, not worth my soul. In true teenage defiance, I joined the masses on Earth, escaping between droplets of rain to become like every other hopeless ground-scurry at the mercy of their corporate overlords. Corporations are no different from your mafia families, where the bonds are tight and bondage even tighter.

The best decision I ever made was becoming a Finder, acquiring whatever people wanted, and fulfilling fetishes without giving a shit about what the objects I collected were for. Correction, acquiring a facial reconstruction cyber mask, my personalized FRCM, from a questionable Omni source, now that was the best decision I ever made. With the morphing of my face into an almost thirty-year-old guy from Arc-Erox, no one recognized or messed with me. If only they knew the identity of the skinny girl beneath the cyber mask.

I'm not sure if someone would go full Event-Horizon drug-overdosed cysycs on me, but I figured most would cower in fear to hear my actual name. Unfortunately, I make a pretty fine ransom so the identity remains a secret, and my dating life complicated to non-existent. On the bright side, as Sandy, I got freedom.

Until today, when I discovered a vile plot during an exchange; Tekeryi Mars-colonies, I hope you receive this broadcast before it's too late. The year is 2220 and the coastline dam didn't break. I repeat my name is Astari Sandy Tekeryi, and the coastline on Earth…it hasn't changed.

THE DAY BEGINS

Let me rewind to what led to this broadcast.

My day starts off with the usual routine. The node in my brain wakes me at 6 a.m., around when the Maglev trains power up and spaceship shuttles start boosting toward the Moon base and Mars colonies. I relieve my-self the female way on a squat pot at the foot of my bed, and then swallow-spit the Rinse Shine for minty breath and chemical-clean teeth into a bucket. On the squat pot's tank are Sud Wipes, which I use to wash.

My contact lens implants play the ad, "Water doesn't wash; let liquid wipes mask the musk." I gag, down the green drink called Ageless Elixir in a neon flask beside my bed, while the Sud Wipe's jingle contin-ues to ring in my head. Everything I use is a luxury, which takes months to afford and collect. Not sure why, but something about how the LED lights lit the sky-scraper buildings on the route home last night makes me want to go all out today.

I stick on the transparent FRCM hidden in a box under my bed, selecting the first game of the day linked to the node in my brain. Second, if you count the Ready-Set-Go app for getting to work on time. I've hit the top ten chart for five days straight, which is disap-pointing if you consider I, as Astari, helped beta-test most of it. Anyway, it's the easiest method to make some side credits, and continue affording my dinky cof-fin-box of freedom.

I grab my favorite Pick-a-Wig off the mannequin's head protruding out the wall closest to my front door. It matches the small silver loop earring in my ear respon-sible for controlling my FRCM without anyone noticing. Also, few around here have real hair these days; most ground-marlers shave it off to avoid the lice. I like my Pick-a-Wig with onyx black Punk spikes, neon blue center, and dark purple shimmer-line highlighting the cyan.

Out of the FRCM's box, I rummage for my clip-on Etch-Sketch black nails, classic skulls on a dog-tag neck chain, black leather wrist straps, and an upgraded tattoo installer to save me time from running to the store. It's a Finder's must-have to keep funds safe and out of the cyber-hackers' greedy claws, or big brother Tekeryi satellites and spying surveillance cameras. To avoid the cameras, as kids, my twin brothers and I would often escape to underground towers; we called them 'reverse skyscrapers.' Don't mock, I was twelve, and my brothers Ferico and Gerig were ten.

My parents' bodyguards never found us, but the lecture was always the same; "Tekeryi must uphold tradition, for we are the eyes of planet Earth and outer space." In memory of the twins' birthday, I pick a double circle tattoo: canine teeth outline and the inside galaxy colored with a barely-visible square barcode for scanning. My one shirt, pair of pants, and shoes; they're made with Tech-wave technology. It's as if the ocean is rippling across my body.

The mirror option in my contacts shows a man's face, but for safety sake should the FRCM glitch, I grab my pill compact. The digestible pink and red globules paint my lips, beige for my skin, and pitch black eyebrows, lashes, and liner. No look is complete without my spiked biker jacket. It's Culio's, an ex; a good guy with a gorgeous smile.

If not on Mars, you'll find my Romeo banished and living on the Moon. I check my points; the vintage jacket pushes me to top five among the marlers. A few more days of this and I figure I can afford to install an actual window rather than rely on a projected landscape to paint my walls with some artificial color. If my daily routine doesn't sound like much, consider how so many take these little things, which make life bearable, for granted.

Also, why do something daily if it has no meaning and isn't worth saving?

I've got time for this podcast broadcasting; as far as the world knows, Sandy just died and Astari is already gone, presumed dead. Keep listening, Martians. I'll get to what led to my death, and no, I'm not dead yet. Soon, I guess, probably by the time you get this broadcast if you're out there listening, Culio.

ARC RAIN

I kiss the door of my room goodbye with two fingers and make my way to the ground floor of the coffin-box, Arc Poverty Tower 11, using the cannon elevator. The speeding death trap lands with a thud and the door creaks open. One hundred stories isn't a lot, but the ear popping is always a bitch. As usual, Buffalo is on the corner, waiting for me outside.

At this point I'm still not sure if the old man is my mentor, handler, or enemy playing some twisted long con. He drinks his anti-worm coffee; the Styrofoam leaks droplets as the murky rain splatters into the cup. I can't describe the flavor for a million credits. The closest maybe is wet dirt, more geosmin than petrichor.

"Am I cursed?" My voice intervenes with the sound of drizzling. "I go outside and it always rains."

Buff doesn't flinch, and seems as uninterested as his scruffy button-up coat. "We're by the coast, new or not, of course it's going to fucking rain."

"Two hundred years doesn't make it new, Buff." I grunt and spit; it's the manliest thing I can think of. "I guess you're right about it having an effect on our Arc city though."

Buff scoffs, chucks his brown-green swill at a gutter, and pushes me to walk ahead of him. "Some Arc," he says. "I wonder if our ancestors knew what they would be saving."

I try to swallow a girlish giggle with a grin, "If they could foretell saving your sorry ass, I'm sure they would've changed their minds."

"Oh, well, excuse me Mister Handsome we can't all afford such a pretty Pick-a-Wig."

Buff amuses me. I'm unable to bite my tongue, and say, "The baldness suits you, but I hope after today's score you can at least afford a Stubble-free."

The old goat groans, "Now there's a jingle they need to send to a black hole in deep space."

There are six blocks of poverty houses to pass; each covered in Tetris-style billboards full of ads in every language known to humankind. I'm bored and start humming, "Stubble-free, stubble-me, I want to be less stubble-ly."

Buff gives me the eye like he's about to pop me a punch to the shoulder. "Kid, if you want to live, I'd suggest you shut the fuck up."

I've got him now, I think, and risk the Maglev rails to reach the opposite sidewalk, singing, "Stubble-free, stubble-me."

In the distance I can hear Buff, "I hate you; I would feed you to a clone dog, no a dino-saber-saurus hybrid."

I chuckle and yell, "Stubble-free…"

"One more syllable and I'm selling you to the wilds as a happy-maggot-meal!"

The rear view image in my contact lens shows Buffalo charging over the Maglev tracks in my direction. The poor dumb bastard trips over the last track and I laugh louder than I've ever allowed myself.

My sweet Martians, maybe you had to be there, but this is what I'm asking you to save, cloud nine.

PACKAGE DELIVERED

I rub my shoulder from Buff's supposed light tap, and open the steel gate to the warehouse between Poverty Tower 4 and 5. The one floor, ground building, was abandoned centuries ago by my father as punishment for the marlers who rioted against the Tekeryi industry. Many families continue to grieve Taken Tuesday, the day my family's company chose to coerce hundreds of young fertile couples and plant them on Moon and

Mars bases, never to return home.

Buffalo's daughter was one of the kids sent to the Moon sometime soon after my father banished you there, Culio. I miss you, and La Luna taunts me each night. I'd shoot her from the night sky if I could, and steal you away from the marriage my father forced you into. I sound like Buffalo, wallowing in a well of self-despair.

Buffalo, when drunk, will mutter he didn't fight hard enough to save his daughter, and the regret pours out with every shot of unfiltered gin he dehydrates his past-prime gut with. I'm not sure what keeps him going outside of being a Finder. His daughter never made it to the Moon base. Kaela's shuttle blew up mid-air and flattened a Tekeryi tower built for the elite.

I remember the shuttle number was 3929, because it would've killed my grandmother had she been on time to meet a friend in the area. Buff might act numb, but I know the number makes him smile. What better revenge could a marler like him get against a Tekeryi? The warehouse is as cold as the memory; I always hated the smell of it.

Rust, dust, and lingering paint fumes. There is a shabby crane on the roof, but nobody with smarts sits on it to move the thing; not worth the tetanus shot. The shots around here cost a literal arm and a leg. We don't make enough as Finders, which is one of the reasons we always get to the meet earlier than our clients, and leave Hasty to bring the goods.

Hasty is a skinny, shady, lanky-looking guy. He could run, which about summed up his talents. The kid lived on tobacco, old-style. He wanted to experience cancer, and boy was he going to get it.

Can't blame Hasty, fifteen and his parents sent to Mars. I know my next words deserve a middle finger from Hasty's parents, but I am sorry. It's not an excuse, but few get to choose the life they're given or their family. I suppose in a way, eventually I did.

I picked the marlers, and chose to fight for the Hastys and

Kaelas.

"Sandy, I got the briefcase," Hasty huffs and puffs.

I hated how he would sneak in past the gate, through the front door, and yell my name for all the silence to hear it. "Shh, we've been over this, you gotta come in quiet," I tell him.

Buff yanks the case covered in ads out of Hasty's hand, "He doesn't know what a guy holding a gun does to a body comes running in yelling."

"Uh, right, but you both don't hold no guns," Hasty checks, his hazel eyes show me he's as scattered as his freckles. The kid struggles to hold up his baggy ripped jeans under his yellow-stained white shirt.

"You gotta think steps ahead, and assume someone unexpected is watching," I lecture Hasty. "Anyway, you did good, now get running before the clients get here."

"Sandy, I need credits, can't wait till end of this week. Don't got no toos for no more food and a coat." I know the kid is hungry; I feel responsible for him, even though he isn't mine. I justify not feeding him more because I can't keep up with his tall build's metabolism, but the truth is Hasty's got too big of a heart, and as a Finder, I can't afford the marler orphans he shelters.

Buff on the other hand has nothing left to lose. He glares at me with his two unforgiving pupils like I'm some heartless asshole, and gives Hasty the coat he's wearing. "What the fuck's a toos?"

"Credits tattoo," I answer Buff, as my fingers unlock the briefcase. I risk a single knee to the cold hard cement and open the case on the ground.

"Sandy, I don't got no toos…"

"Here, Hasty take this, it's the last spare toos I got on me. Now get. You leave the rest to us. Meetings are no place for a child." I cave, and ruffle up Hasty's knotted hair. His matted locks give the sensation of touching some combination of cobwebs, hay, and carpet. The boy grins rotten teeth at me and rubs his ginger mess, mimicking my hand movements over his hair, and then speeds off.

Buff shakes his head like he can't figure me out. "How do you have an extra credit tattoo in your possession?"

Old Buffalo's got my heart thumping in my ears to the point I feel as though my contacts are gonna pop themselves out. I need an answer, and use the delay to play it cool with a lie, "It's an empty shell."

"You'd give a poor, starving, and homeless orphaned runner who works for us a shell? What? Does Hasty's loyalty mean nothing to you?"

"Don't, Buff, just don't. What good are we doing him if he gets too dependent on us? Feed him today, something happens, what you gonna give him tomorrow? Part with all you've got and then when you got nothing more to give, go beg for mercy from some other poor marler? You know citizens belonging to Tekeryi and the other corporations won't give you shit."

"I want nothing from them, and I'd sell my skin so long as it means I don't become them." Buff breathes the last words hot down my neck, like he knows who I am. "Case done," he grumbles, shoving my head forward.

"Yeah, case done. The package is in good condition and ready for our clients." I say, getting off the cracked marble, because there's nothing worse for our business image than a client seeing a ground-marler kneel on the ground.

PANDORA S BRIEFCASE

Buff and I hear the gate clatter. The front door swings open to the warehouse, with hidden exits and a back door to a torn-up yard. In stomps two black-marketers built for never-to-be-mentioned fight clubs. The voice of the black-marketer behind them is the churned milk powder to our daily preservative-caked bread.

"Sandy and my favorite Buffet. How are my two finest Finders in the kingdom belonging to our ever present industrial masters, hmm?"

"Sockumn. What clone-beast did you skin to end up with such a fine looking fur?" I placate, and then elbow Buff as he coughs, "scrotum," under his breath. The problem with Buff's age is he no longer cares about insulting our business clients. Sockumn and I work together often; he has a thing for my male face, and I figure it's why he lets Buff's insult slide.

"Oh, this dusty cloak? She was a fine creature. Smokey tails, five of them, weren't there, Makey?"

"Yes boss, five."

"Five. The perkiest little ears, small for such a big beast, but Sandy, oh, Sandy you should've seen her claws. Majestic. From the tip of each jutted nail-bone lines ran up to and around her hybrid mane. Keef is wearing a couple, sanded and re-designed of course. Keef, show Sandy your holster."

Keef, a man without front teeth, does as his boss asks, and it's a sore sight. My gut wrenches for the creature. The thought of it being stuck through a fur processor, not given a chance, no hunt, just Sockumn's moisturized fingers pointing out to the zookeeper, which to slaughter.

"Nice teeth, Keef," Buff smirks. Sockumn catches the offensive joke and giggles, whereas Keef, clueless, continues to display his boney-holster. Buff gives me the eye to prepare for a brawl, because he knows hidden behind the charade is a threat of Sockumn's force.

"So who do I have to thank for my prize? Who procured this darling briefcase for me," Sockumn asks.

"I'm a Walker cyber technician, Elema."

Our next guest enters from behind Sockumn. I can tell from the swing of her hips she thinks Sockumn's interest is in her curves. She doesn't realize he wants her ruby-feathered shoes, and not the owner wearing them. Elema didn't have to be present at the meeting; she'd given us the briefcase with the item Sockumn wanted.

Buff and I had verified the contents of the briefcase were intact, but regardless of the technology and runners available, Finder meetings require non-virtual contact. Credits don't enter accounts until buyers meet their sellers. Those who try meetings without Finder middlemen and women often end up in a shoot-out or thrown to the fringe on the other side of the four main corporations' protective walls. Sometimes the elite would seek to hunt those living in the fringe or further out in the wilds for the purposes of cloning.

My twin brothers loved watching the hunts on livestream in our house. Catcher's Day, they nicknamed it, and much to my parent's disapproval, I hated Catcher's Day.

Yeah Martians, your shit is bad, but it isn't the worst.

"I will set up the projection here so you can watch the video on this wall," Elema says.

Her pencil-skirt leaves little to the imagination when she bends over. Buff, the gentleman, tries not to ogle and keeps his attention on Makey and Keef, while Sockumn's still got his hawk eye on her pumps. Elema flicks a strand of hair at Sockumn; disregarding the danger she's putting herself in. I stand by in odd amusement of the scene.

The video played and my sweet Martians that damn thing, it's why you're receiving my broadcast twenty-three hours after I woke up today.

Every graph, well-known scientist, you name it, popped up with propaganda news displaying how the dam broke. Waters from old DC to old NY flood the area, while pre-recorded lies discuss the threat of another new coastline. A plot meant to afford the four leading corporations ground, which they could use to further develop cybernetics and bioaugmentation. Step-by-step the instructions show how to incite panic and push the poor past the point of submission to their dominating corporate overlords.

Here on the ground as a marler, I'd experienced it. It, whatever it is, it isn't slavery. I can't think of a word heinous enough to describe such acts by people meant to rule with a sense of dignity and responsibility. People like my family whose rationale I comprehend even if I don't always agree with their MO.

I think of Buff who has no one, losing…can a person like him lose more? Hasty doesn't deserve such a future, and knowing him, he wouldn't abandon the marler-orphans in his care. He'd try and survive the dam break only to be executed by Sweepers. Yeah, Sweepers, "the new job for the loyal citizen making way for a brighter future."

The bastards already had a jingle for their fucking plan. What hurt the worst; it isn't the excited look on Sockumn's face to be the one to deliver the updated plans from Walker to Tekeryi. My contacts zoom in on two signatures, in the bottom right corner, in tiny handwriting.

PRIDE & POWER

Full credit for coming up with the original idea went to my twin baby brothers. In my head, I heard Ferico's and Gerig's most adorable laughter, drowned out by marlers' harrowing screams. The image of my innocent brothers replaced with two grown men standing amidst an ocean of blood and trampled bodies. I might as well have been the sister of Makey and Keef.

How is it I share the same bloodline as two such monsters?

Buff must have been watching me; I'd slipped up and placed my hand, too feminine, over my mouth rather than clenching a concealed fist. It's a stupid reflex, covering my mouth while saying my brothers' nicknames, Ferry & Gerry.

"You're paler than a woman's white skin globule from a pill compact, keep it together," Buff whispers in my ear. I thank the universe my FRCM hides what has to be red eyes from the feverish rage I can feel frying my forehead. I glare, nod, and stand up straight.

"Is there perhaps a doozy you've noticed you would like to share with us, darling Buffet?"

"No, Sockumn. I was discussing with my young partner here that given the content of the product you might be wantin' to pay up couple more credits than agreed upon."

Elema switches off the projector, packs up her case, and huffs, "Finders are not to negotiate funds after discovery…"

"Hush, Elema dear, you aren't anywhere near as rich as you think you are."

"Oh, ha, ha. I'm wealthy enough to make you jealous. It will do. Make sure Tekeryi gets the plans, Sockumn. No one else or both corporation families will be out to hunt you."

Hunt! Catcher's Day, that's what must've inspired my brothers. I block out Sockumn and Elema's miniature feud, focusing more on whether or not my brothers realized their actions weren't part of some game.

"Oh, Elema, you're a snarky one aren't you?" Sockumn's honeyed voice brings me to the present once again. "Here are your credits, hope it helps get you laid," Sockumn pats Elema's shoulder before she storms out the door, and then pops the artificial-whalebone ribbing in his fur collar.

Makey and Keef respond by drawing their weapons, blocking the front door exit. Buff doesn't bat either green eye, but rather strokes his brown and white stubble with a hand in a manner similar to shrugging shoulders as if the situation wasn't worth comment. It doesn't matter what the contents of the briefcase are or how they vex Buff and I. Survival requires us to be diplomatic until the business meeting concludes.

Sockumn opens his fur coat to reveal the lines of torture devices tucked inside, "Now what's this about you wanting more credits for doing your job?"

"Buff asked me about more credits, but we're both honorable Finders. If you're satisfied with the product then we're happy to have provided service with honesty, full disclosure, and a smile," I tug on my earring so the FRCM displays the most suitable expression for such a delicate situation.

"Sandy, you dear thing. All right, you've won my heart. I can't suffer to see such dark sadness in your eyes."

"You're not without compassion, Sockumn."

"Now, now, Sandy, there's no need...although, I will accept an apology from Buffet. A heartfelt one, if capable."

Buff shakes his head, and glares at Sockumn. The two men in their forties have locked horns, as it sometimes goes. Makey hiccups, Keef yawns, and I wait. It's on Buff if we get to walk, and for a minute I fear not making it.

He has to say one word, Sockumn isn't asking much, but pride is an egocentric thing.

Buff rolls his eyes, irons out his brown marler clothes with a hand, nods his head, and says, "I'd rather have brought some hybrid bones to sell yuh, but yeah, sure, sorry."

"Don't tell me I managed to get the great tough Buff to apologize?" Sockumn claps with excitement.

I don't dare move; not wanting to upset the balance, and flummoxed by how well Buff knows what to say and do to get us out of a fight with the black-marketers. "Dispute's not worth getting shot at," grumbles the old goat.

"You have to pick your battles, as my uncle used to

say. Ha! I do enjoy picking every one of them."

"You're a strange one Sockumn," says Buff, but I have a feeling everyone in the room, including Sockumn, agrees with the statement.

Sockumn smirks, "Why spill your blood when I can scotch your macho reputation? Here are my credits you're so eager to get your grubby, hairy paws on. Consider it hush money, Buffet, for the secrets you and the boy must now keep."

Sockumn grabs the case Hasty had brought so Buff and I wouldn't be blamed for tampering, and laughs himself hysterical out the front door. Makey pushes past Keef who is trailing behind his boss to flaunt his bone holster straps at me for as long as possible. I pass half the credits Sockumn wired to me on to Buff, agreeing to cover the full expense and pay Hasty his ten percent share later in the week.

Don't worry Martians and Hasty's parents; if you're listening, before sending this broadcast I wired all the credits in my possession as Sandy and Astari over to Hasty. He can experience cancer, make a complete recovery, reconstruct his entire body, own a rich Tekeryi tower, and house every single marler orphan for free if he wants. If he can run fast enough to live. I'll explain soon enough.

A COFFEE CUP OF DEATH

"Buffalo, you ready to go? It's 10 a.m. Jabala's should be open. Cup of the best boiled coffee beans, on me?"

"Buffalo…what parent names their child after a creature that's extinct? Ugh, and stupid scrotum. If I see him and he calls me Buffet one more time I'm going to present him with the biggest buffet of knuckle sandwiches he's…"

"Buff, puff it out. It's steady head ahead, remember?"

"Yeah, yeah, smart ass," Buff mutters and then

getting to the metal gate says to me, "Ladies first." He says it every time, but little does Buff know Sandy doesn't exist and Astari Tekeryi, his enemy, is the girl beneath the imperceptible FRCM.

We get to Jabala's Feffy & Co. coffee house between Poverty Tower 7 and 8 at around 11 a.m. Three androids own Jabala's as equal partners; Jabalapopa, Jabalaboba, and Jabalakoka. The business and androids are named after their android creator the artificially intelligent coffee machine Jabala, of course. Buff and I came across the place two years back.

We sit on the same stools every time, once a week, and order the same anti-worm Styrofoam cup filled with sludge. Most androids experience glitches and are liable to kill a percentage of their customers, but not at Jabalas. I remember near a month passed until Buff spilled his cup over Jabalapopa by accident and commented, "Oh look! An android not trying to kill someone, that's new." The comment about safety made us regulars, because the coffee swill sure as hell isn't worth the credits.

The wind had picked up since the morning, but the rain slowed to about a trickle. Ads, against the windowless walls of the coffin-box and honeycomb-shaped B-apartments, project into the street. From microscopic to larger than life, the view in the working hours of the day is packed. Virtual beings block any sense of a spacious view, towering over rich and poor citizens alike.

"Welcome to Jabala's." The projected android's voice is as welcome as the glitch-prone signs to the storefront.

Same as every other store, the outside is a cylinder of bamboo rings with the menu running in a neon sign on the innermost pillar, viewable between the outer rings. Grandfather Beard moss hangs over the sides and oak tree pillars tie inner cylinder to cylinder. You can smell the oxygen, but never make out its source. I know the source because as a Tekeryi descendant, it's important for me to understand how Tekeryi-owned industries are designed.

A waste of time and knowledge, considering what my brothers, Ferico and Gerig, had helped create. I enter Jabala's ahead of Buff and sit by the corner displaying a landscape of flowers under a bright Sun.

"Sandy, Buffalo, are we willing to try something new today? We have a Martian special, Red Spice Latte. I have tried it; the caffeine boost activates the node in a remarkable way. Stronger than a regular, bit of a Fire Hat without the nasty side effects."

"Nah thanks Jabalapopa. I think I'll stick with the regular and avoid the off chance I start an Event-Horizon addiction."

"Very well, Sandy. How about you, Buffalo, would you care for a trip off-world?"

"You know what Popa, unlike my coward of a friend here, I think I'm going to risk it." First red flag. Buff might've not had much to live for but he's always cautious. I shrug it off, thinking he's shaken by the plans we'd seen.

"I think this is one of the few places which don't force a person to order by selecting what they want from those ad-filled pop-ups that display on cyber-glasses."

"It does have a nice human touch to it, Buff."

"I'm gonna miss this place." Second red flag. Again, I think Buff is referencing the corporation's plans to induce widespread panic by tricking everyone into believing we're about to lose the dam and have ourselves a new coastline.

"Buff, we can stop this from happening." I shut my mouth quick when Buffalo kicks my shin as Jabalaboba and Jabalakoka hover, ejecting trays with our respective orders from their Styrofoam coffee-cup-designed android bodies.

Buff waits for the two to leave, and says to me, "Oh, after today, we won't be seeing this place again, Sandy." Third red flag. I'm starting to make out something's not quite right. Buff isn't staring off at the landscape, he isn't spinning his cup, and his voice has changed from baritone to something deeper.

I bite the bait, sip my sludge, pretending all is well, and say, "Alright Buff, you wanna hijack a shuttle and head for Mars before this place turns to whatever is worse than hell?"

"I'm sure the Tekeryi family has something in store for their pretty little offspring so they don't end up on a shithole like Mars." Fourth red flag. I can't react. There's a slim chance Buff hasn't figured out my identity, and is choosing to rag me for old times' sake.

"Buff, what has gotten into you?"

"Cut the bullshit, Sandy, if that's even your name. Runaway daughter. No! No you don't get to look shocked. I knew you weren't a guy, but it wasn't until you whispered pet names for Ferico and Gerig that I figured out you're a fucking abomination. A Tekeryi. You think a little tech could hide you? Make-up and clothes won't make you a man. A guy doesn't have to think about being a guy, he just is. You're a disgrace. What you come live here for, huh? What? Did you think living with marlers could erase who you are?"

I don't respond, my heart pounding. I can't move. Buff is going to betray me, but I can't blame him since I'd betrayed him first. He'd adopted me, I realize too late, as a daughter.

Only to discover I belong to the enemy responsible for ending his daughter's life.

I guess it's why I don't react when he says, "Goodbye, Sandy."

A bullet hits my side, and the Jabala androids come to my defense. The oversized cups' eyes blink in Morse. I decode the message; it seems my brothers had programmed the androids to watch out for me after figuring out where I'd gone and hid. A way to keep tabs on me, a sign they miss me, I guess.

It doesn't change my anger at their plans to unite the corporations by focusing on driving out thousands of people. With marlers fleeing the coffee shop, Buff distracted in a gun war with the Jabalas, and my blood pouring out, I act on instinct after Buff's stray bullet from his no-longer-secret-pocket-pistol grazes and cracks my mask. I swallow the globules in my pill compact, which isn't fun when you've been shot. The globules cover my face in make-up so I can remove my FRCM.

I have to get home to my coffin-box. I have an emergency medical kit stuffed in my mattress, but I don't have a weapon or the heart to kill Buff. I don't know how Jabalakoka's gun got in my hand, how I found the strength to lift it, and aim it at Buff's forehead after he killed the Jabala androids. I remember the tears, standing over Buff's dead body, one kill shot.

Every emotion screamed in my head, but cold as ice, I remember covering his eyes. I don't remember how I stumbled to my place. In a blur of agony, I must have walked in the rain awhile, my Pick-a-Wig's spikes flowed long hair around my shoulders. I don't know where I got the blade to slice my thin mattress, and inject myself with nanobots to help congeal and seal my gun wound from losing more blood. I somehow manage to make copies from the flash drive where I'd copied over the corporation's plans.

I had to warn everyone. Hasty's help to find a local doctor was essential, but first I needed sleep and collapse.

HOPE HIDDEN IN A GAP

I've no idea how long I was out; it was after 3 p.m. according to my internal node watch. I cough, use a wipe, change the setting on my clothes to paint-splatter as a cover for the blood stains, and yeah I was smart enough to make copies of cases I got as a Finder. There's a hollowness, which follows betrayal and more than a bullet, it shatters a person's insides.

I wonder if this is how my family felt when I ran away from them, if this is how the marlers would feel learning about the corporation's plans, and if this is how you felt, Hasty's parents. You, Martians, better than anyone know what it means to be betrayed by the powers you trusted in. I don't hold it against you, and I don't blame Buff for trying to kill me, but at the same time a part of me hopes my family survives. It's twisted, all of it, and there are no right words or answers.

I'm not going to be able to make up for the past, but I hope that with this broadcast, maybe the future can be better than yesterday. Anyway, I'm sharing some of the things I thought about when I caught one of the four Maglevs to a gap between two bamboo stores.

The gap is a place nearest the edge of the wall protecting us from the fringe and wilds outside. The bamboo rings protruding over the alley in the gap make for a roof where Hasty and some orphans stay. I try not to clutch my side during the ride, but the medical kit's black-market painkillers have worn off. Sockumn's cheap brand of opioids, I figure.

Two kids in layers of tattered clothes and no shoes sit at the entrance, guarding the gap, their alley home. My timing, uncalculated, but perfect as I spot Hasty carrying cases of leftovers from the Freeze Dried Tarts bakery on the left side of the gap.

Now you know, Martians, in case you ever get the chance to come and find him, he's on the corner of an intersection, and next door to a LED and Optics light store. I'm guessing the stores are what keep the kids warm, being nearby.

My throat is hoarse from crying on the train, but I call out to Hasty. I forgot I wasn't wearing the FRCM anymore, and yell out the name Sandy to the confused look on his face. He scratches his head and keeps walking. The two big kids by the gap's entrance stand up ready to defend Hasty from me.

Desperate, I cross the tracks and street then yell Hasty's real name. "Hastins!"

"How do you know my name, Miss?"

I don't have the time to explain and say, "Buffalo killed Sandy." It wasn't a lie; I mean the bastard did crack my mask.

"What?" Hasty almost drops the crates, fumbles the lot in his hands, and then passes them to his friends, ordering them to feed the kids inside. It's a side of him I've not seen before, a leader.

"My name is…" I need a new identity, same node, but once again a different name.

"Your name is?"

"Astari." I figure there's no hiding it anymore. I can have him say my name, and not believe I'm a Tekeryi because the forty-eight hour pill compact globules hide the image the marlers know from the missing person's ads. My father had filled countless billboards with the least photogenic pictures of myself the day I ran away from home.

"Astari? How you know Buff killed Sandy? Buff would never done that, nopes, I'm sorry Miss. I don't believe you."

"Hastins, it's on the news, I'm sure the scrapers will display what happened here soon, but I need your help."

"Miss, you're not making much sense, and I got hungry marlers to feed."

"The briefcase this morning. The corporations are plotting to work together and lie about the weather creating a new coastline so marlers will panic and run to the fringe. The corporations want the land to build new industries. Sandy made a copy, he trusted me with his last breath to get this to you, he needs you to deliver it to the border."

"Miss, corporations don't hate marlers, they need us, they would never do stuff like you're talkin'. Let's say I believe yuh, why would Buff go and shoot Sandy? Buff is like Sandy's daddy."

"Hasty, Buff…Buffalo didn't want Sandy to reveal the plans, it's against the Finder's oath."

"You're a real bad day, Miss Astari. A real bad day."

"Look here, see my side bleeding? I barely got away after Buffalo started shooting. I don't know, maybe someone drugged his Jabala coffee."

I need Hasty to hurry up and help me before the news displays my half-truth and lies. One last time I had to lean on the kid's good heart. He'd be hailed a hero for it, which is how I justify my actions.

DOCTOR WARPATH

I wouldn't be surprised if you think the worst of me, Martians, but if we're being honest, you and Hasty's parents hate me anyway. I'm not asking you to forgive and save me, but Hasty, he deserves your help. He might be the one decent person and last remnant of humanity left in the world, a caring, and tobacco-chewing, skinny marler orphan. Someone as pure as this kid, I can't believe he shed tears for me, for Sandy.

Hasty sniffles and wipes his puffy eyes, trying to hide his flushed face from the tiny bodies staring out from the darkness of the gap. "I'll do the runnin'. Sandy broke an oath, but he don't deserve no shootin' for it. Sandy's one who found me near this gap, lying beaten, and he offered me a runnin' job. He always paid me extra credits than I deserved, I wasn't no good in the beginning but Sandy stuck by me. Ima sure miss seein' his fancy Pick-a-Wig, and I see he gave you his favorite biker's jacket."

"Yeah Hasty, he did, but the copy isn't the only thing he told me to give you before he died. He wanted you to have his coffin-box, Pick-a-Wigs, and credits too."

"Miss, it's too much, I can't. I can't do that. Why don't you keep some of it?"

"Hasty, you got a heart purer than platinum, you know. I don't need anything but to get fixed up by a proper doctor."

"Oh yeah, you're hurt bad ain't yuh. Here, come with me, there's a doctor I know. She real proper, name's old Sally, she'll help you out. She lives above her office down at the end of this here alley. I'll take you."

Hasty keeps his word and pulls a blanket, which smells of mold and mothballs, over my head as he leads me through the gap. "Pardon the blanket Miss, but don't want no young marlers gettin' frightened what with your blood leakin' through your shirt. All these kids ever see is blood. In the gap, their home, they don't deserve to see more of it."

We got to old Sally's around five minutes later, about 4 p.m. She isn't old, but at twenty, she's older than the kids hiding in the gap. Through Sally and her gentle nature I realize her practice, the owners of Freeze-dried, LED, and a flower shop protect those in the gap from Tekeryi surveillance and Gatter law enforcement. Sally wears blue everything, and a white flower fan in her ponytail to symbolize she's a doctor.

Ten metal stripes on a fan means the best, and Sally has eight. Hasty whispers something to her, hugs me tight, and sprints for the fringe to relay the news to a man at the border named Bobcat. Bob was half wild and half fringe, but the guards like him and so allow him to cross the wall now and then at the cost of wild game meats. I met Bobcat through Buff when a buyer had asked for a large amount of credits for some of the gamey meat.

Bobcat and I didn't get along great when we met. I may have been moody that day and asked if he had a tail to go with the name. I'm counting on his hatred for Tekeryi surveillance and Gatter law enforcement to get news of the corporation's plans out as far widespread as possible. On Bobcat's copy of the plans, I added back door secrets into the Tekeryi towers security system should he need it.

I wave at Hasty as he runs out of Sally's office, without a coat, likely toward my coffin-box for the credits, then on to the wall and tail-less Bobcat.

"He is a good kid, isn't he," Sally says.

"The best," I agree.

"Lie on your back on the flat chair. Good. Oh my, such a terrible wound, who shot you? Sorry, never mind, Hasty said no questions, but I have got to say, I sure am curious."

"Why do you help Hasty?" I ask Sally.

"He is a born hero, pulled me out when there was a gas leak and called for help when no one else bothered. If it were not for him my practice and I would have gone up in flames."

"Wow."

"Right! Since then, whenever he needs a favor I do my best to help him in any way I can. I do not wish to upset the corporations, especially Gatter law enforcement, but there is something I cannot resist about his tobacco smile. Although, Hasty needs to stop chewing the stuff, I keep telling him it is laced with pesticide, fantasied, and other sides. Can you believe the boy wants to experience cancer? I mean woman to woman, it is strange, right?"

"Woman to woman? Oh, yeah, I mean yes it's sure strange."

I've been pretending to be a marler guy so long I almost forgot who I was. Sandy had been such a big part of my life. Unable to talk about myself as him, it felt as though he had lived and Buff had killed him, not just the mask. I try to imagine what my, what Sandy's funeral would be like.

Would Hasty risk Tekeryi surveillance to send my body, Astari's body, off in the incinerator?

I mourn the thought of dying alone, forgotten by you, Culio. Also, hated or not much known by everyone I'd met outside my Tekeryi family.

"Oh dear, I am sorry, am I hurting you? Do you need a wipe for your eyes, hun?"

"No, thank you Sally, I am alright."

"I am about done, a little longer, and your internals and externals should be stitched up. You will need rest. Any stress or exertion will open the wound and require surgery. Oh, and Hasty calls me Sally because he cannot say my name without mispronouncing it. Although, I wish he would stop calling me old. Anyway, I mean, I don't mind if you call me Sally, but in case you were wondering my name is Saldalina."

"Thank you for the stitches, Saldalina. I'm Astari."

Yes, Martians, I risk it and tell her my name. Maybe the blood loss sapping my energy is the reason I'm not bothered with forming a new identity.

"Astari? Pretty name. Astari, Ah-star-ee, where do I know…oh my, you cannot-you cannot be!"

"I am."

"Astari Tekeryi? She disappeared. I don't mean to be rude, but everyone presumed she, I mean you, died."

"No, I ran away, and became a Finder," I tell her.

"You do not look like the photos of Astari," Sally says.

"Pill compact, and you can run my blood through the database, but I must warn you my family will hunt you if you do."

"I, um, have a database disconnected from the corporations' surveillance, since we're sharing secrets. Why do you trust me with this? I mean, thank you, but why?"

"You will understand when I hand you a copy of the plans the corporations want to implement, which will push scrapers and marlers out to the fringe and wilds. It's a plan meant to enrich the lives of the rich and enslave the poor even further."

"You are lying, I mean you must be lying, the Tekeryi family especially would never do such a thing. The Tekeryi family protects us from the other corporations, and from the outside. I mean yes, my system shows you are Astari, somehow, but then you hate your family so why should I believe you?"

"I don't hate them, but I don't agree with what they're doing. My brothers designed the plans, if anything I blame Catcher's Day. Do you know the hunting ritual?"

"Not the name as such, but yes, I know the wealthy hunt fringe and wild radicals to keep us safe."

"No, we hunt, my family hunts captured innocents and kills or clones them for sport."

"Despicable, if what you are saying is true, but I do not want to believe it."

"Why else would I run away, a Tekeryi royal if you will, to become this, a marler?"

"So the Tekeryi who care about us is you, and not your family, is what you are saying?"

"You can see the plans for yourself, but I have no reason to con you. I do need your help to warn the middle and wealthy classes who will be affected as well. Forget my family and the elite. We deserve what's coming our way. Make a future for Hasty."

"You must be a princess; you can name but one soul to save, and expect me to drop everything and carry out your plans for you. What is the marler's word for a rich person? Up-scraper? You are an up-scraper, scraping away those you feel are beneath you to claw your way to the top of the elite tower."

"If you don't share the copy of the files with the corporations plot…"

"Stop it, just stop it. Sorry for my temper, but you test my equity, dropping this in my lap. I know what to do, and I will risk my life for Hasty and everyone who has ever been loyal to a corporation, blinded by the constant brainwashing ads and android-delivered statements."

"Thank you, Saldalina."

"No, do not thank me. Do not thank someone who pities you."

ROOTS BELOW

Saldalina's words crush me as the sound of her footsteps drift out of the office. The silence hits like a gong, and I notice why she doesn't have any other patients or staff members. There on the wall a Gatter stamp glows its daunting black symbol. The one who works here isn't considered good enough by the corporate families to have a practice.

Saldalina spoke as though she'd swallowed the shame of the black symbol as a problem she represented, rather than calling out the corporate leaders like Tekeryi for being a bug on society. Judgment on the Tekeryi name would come; I would be the gavel to a family who had drowned so many by inciting public hatred. I once thought it acceptable to watch the few fall by the wayside, as so many do, even though we're part of the same network. Not getting involved or risk getting caught up in the chaos is pointless, because no one gets to bow out and hide.

Are you hearing me, Martians? Even you so far away, you may be sky sailors, as the marlers name you, but it doesn't mean you get to sail away. What-what am I doing? I've got no right to ask your help.

I guess a part of me knew this because in the flash

drive I handed Saldalina is a virus. I'd encoded it before the meeting with Sockumn and Elema on the off chance I'd need to use it against them. Saldalina's naivety and blind loyalty makes her the perfect candidate to deliver it to Gatter law enforcement and ergo their system. If Saldalina acts as I predict she will, the virus will shut down Gatter operations and give people a chance to riot until Monday.

It's not a lot of time, but a week is what I can buy you Martians. Travel to Earth and make sure the corporations don't endanger more lives.

I feel stuck, even though Saldalina didn't bother to lock up. I stumble out the office on the ground floor, aching, but not ready to give up. I shove my long hair inside my biker jacket.

I mean your jacket, Culio.

It helps hide my hair's length so I can hail a taxi copter at a hail-post by pressing one of those old pedestrian-crossing do-nothing buttons. The android pilot arrives in a tick and then tries to bio-scan read my face, but puffy eyes and the pill compact hide my full signature. The news displays Buff's fight against the Jabala brothers and I everywhere. The worst day, replays on repeat on every screen on every building and device.

The taxi copter itself, holding the wanted suspect, plays the scene on the side of the doors for everyone to see. The taxi copter travels over Arc city then hovers above a helipad parking spot next to the Tekeryi's base headquarters. I must've told the android pilot my name is Sandy when I hopped in. He sure looks confused when the name Astari Tekeryi pops up as he scans the credits from a last-resort tattoo chip my parents embedded under my skin when I was five.

"Don't mind me, but what was an up-scraper girl like you doing in a down world like that, Miss?" The automated statement makes me wonder if the android is flying the helicopter on autopilot.

I take a chance and respond with, "Oh, you know, secret missions and stuff."

I get not a peep out of the machine. Grateful for the luck, I climb out, stand in the middle of the road, and open a manhole in the street to get into an ancient sewer line. For as there are up-scrapers and marlers there are under-grounders and down-rooters. A down-rooter is a mole, blind with a short life span, but these humans can build.

Tekeryi industries own the towers on top, and those beneath Arc city as well. Most of the corporations do, though a limited number of people know they exist. The neon strands woven into my clothes light a faint glow, shining on the homes beneath. I can hear the chattering of the down-rooters teeth.

Mid-way in the main tunnel a human, gender unknown and unidentifiable to marlers and up-scrapers, carries bones around its waist. The person has roots growing out of their skin in various places, the whitest hair, and biggest black pupils. An under-grounder in marler clothes crouches beside the down-rooter, shielding sensitive eyes against the neon light I'm wearing. Other than the pale skin and ring of red around the eyes, the under-grounder could be mistaken for a marler, but we don't say a word to each other.

I hand over a flash drive and they play it on a Walkman-type audio device in front of me. The down-rooter grabs the drive and sprints with heavy steps into a dark tunnel. The under-grounder tells me to wait in sign language, and after disappearing for a few minutes, returns with a marching group of people armed to the teeth. The under-grounder signs a stutter, hesitates, and then points a gun at my head.

I can feel the blood drain as I stagger into a wet puddle formed by the rain dripping down the cracks of the manhole. Oxygen ventilation exists, but I feel short of breath. A person next to the one holding the gun, signs on the gun-holder's face, and reluctantly the gun-holder lowers the rifle. The under-grounder, who signed on the gun-holder to spare my life, clicks and uses echo-location, pointing to their nose and then my wound before signing, "leave," in the air.

The under-grounder must have sensed I'm not long for this world. I struggle to open the manhole, tired, but determined; I jump up and shove myself out to the ground level. I close the manhole from the storm; lightning arcs in the sky, snaking through the dark grey clouds above. I've another copy of the plan to deliver, but this next trip will mean my end.

I know it, but I can't turn back, and I've got nothing left to lose.

THE TEARS OF A UNICORN

The Tekeryi headquarters, with ring houses somewhat visible through the lightning clouds, requires a mandatory elevator ride. The blueprints and access points change along with the building's rotating architecture. I don't have weapons but remember a green toolbox where my mother had made my father keep some for emergencies. In the garage parking lot, hidden in a public restroom with a permanent 'out of order' sign are a door and two bolted windows.

The door is an easy crack but the next two require biometric scanning and an invasive node scan by swallowing a nanobot. Biometrics, they're easy to trick. Even if I'd had to remove my electric dampener in the mask so my node couldn't be tracked, switched off the voice changer in my throat, and taken off the chest-flattening plate I had worn each day as Sandy. If I weren't Astari Tekeryi, the nanobot would kill me.

If ever there was a time to be sure of my identity it was now. I pass the door and first window, but can't bring myself to risk the bot. A voice calls in the distance, asking what I'm doing. Out of time and in need of some basic defense gear, I swallow the bot.

The final window won't open and I wonder how many seconds I have for the bot to activate the kill switch implanted in my node. Ten seconds never passed by so painfully slowly, but they do, and the window displays a flat screen number keypad. I type in the last code I can remember, the lock clicks open, and I dress up in every bit of padding and weaponry available. I don't aim, but heading from the parking lot into the Tekeryi building, with quick glances, fire headshots at the voices.

I could've used backup, but backup is running to the fringe, relaying my message through middle-class social networks, and causing a ruckus underground. I climb the stairs connecting the headquarters to an inner space elevator, and focus on counting the silver linings like Buff had taught me once. First silver lining. The surveillance has blind spots and I know them.

Second silver lining. I make it five flights of stairs before Tekeryi security guards spot me. Third, I'm skilled at close and long-range combat. Fourth, heading for the broadcasting station on the top floor of the space elevator, no more than eight guards fight me inside the elevator on the way up.

Fifth silver lining. I'm not completely shot to pieces by the time I make it to the broadcast station, and jump in a spacesuit to breathe oxygen at a high altitude.

It's as clear and clean as I remember, while watching the view of the storm beneath and stars shining in the distance with you, Culio.

I make it, eliminate the staff, and plug the plans into the system. The signal should broadcast far and wide if nobody shuts down the electricity and generators, risking a citywide blackout, a shitty scenario for Arc city. I think my spacesuit is compressing the wounds; the good news is I'll die slow. The bad news is the same.

Would my parents have risked giving birth to my brothers and me if they could've known what would become of their bloodline? Would they blame themselves or like the marlers point their fingers and place the blame elsewhere? I've either gone and started a citywide riot or failed. What if Bobcat kills Hasty, loyalists turn on Saldalina, and the under-grounder armies, unable to handle the bright neon lights, do not venture above ground?

What if my twin brothers built the plans to start a ruse and flush me out? What if Ferico and Gerig chose to hunt me for Catcher's Day? I don't know. I don't know, and I'm afraid.

Here I am holding on to a last copy for some stranger in case the broadcast doesn't reach. Boy it sucks to cry in a spacesuit.

Teardrops aside, I can still make out the clear sky at least; it's as blue as the hair I was born with. Honest, I came into this world with real blue hair, golden eyes, and albino white lips. I'm a unicorn, my sweet Martians, but my magic is gone, and it's time to cross the rainbow.

Memory full, recording has stopped.

NODE DOWNLOAD COMPLETE

"Astari, it's Culio. I'm here, Astari. My base downloaded your message. I can't believe you managed to keep my jacket after your parents separated us. I'm so proud of you, my Juliet. Hey, I got your message. Astari, are you there?"

NEO[N] BUSHIDO

By Patrick Tillett.

Sounds of the city were muted beyond the walls of Hiro's dojo and the rumble of buildings and billboards alive with electricity were reduced to a rising and falling hum, barely perceptible yet underlying every silence like the bass line to a song that never ended. Hiro enjoyed the solitude as he sipped the steaming green tea from a tin cup. He always took tea while he meditated, letting the simulated sounds of birds, wind rustling through leaves, and distant oceans wash over him from hidden speakers. Sometimes, he was even able to wash away the cold steel world outside and forget that his abode was likely the only place in the Bloc, if not the whole city, that still had honest-to-goodness foliage within its walls.

Urgent rapping on the door snapped his attention back to reality. He whipped open the door, letting in the sounds and smells of the city which he so fervently tried to keep out, and was taken aback by his unexpected visitor.

A girl stood on his doorstep; a child around ten or twelve. Her black hair was matted to her head and rain had pasted her clothes to her small body. She had sharp features. *Latin? Definitely not Japanese*, Hiro observed, *she's not from around here, most likely.* But he kept coming back to the first thing he noticed; she was smoking a long, smelly cigarette. He snatched it from between her lips and tossed it into a puddle of rainwater. She exhaled an odorous cloud in response.

"Little girls should not smoke. Where are your parents?" Hiro asked, cutting to the point.

"Don't have any. I need to come in." Her tone was matter-of-fact, and the girl shrugged to unstick her clothes from her shoulders.

"You may not. Go away." He started to shut the door and nearly had it closed all the way when he suffered a flash of images in quick succession. *Raven hair against the neon light. Cold steel warmed by fresh blood. Children's laughter, and children who would laugh no more. A lonely warrior, wizened by sin.*

He paused. At this moment, on the threshold, the girl knew he would help. She had hoped, of course, but now she knew for sure that Hiro Tarokata, ex-Enforcer for the 1Akuz0 Corporation was her ally. He re-opened the door and wordlessly invited her in.

"My name's Levy by the way, but I need to hide right now because someone is about to come here looking for me." Levy walked past him and ducked aside into one of the cupboards away from the entrance. "Don't tell them I'm here." Hiro shut the door behind her and pensively sipped at his tea, as if in a trance. There was renewed knocking at the door.

This time he was face to face with an android from the 1Akuz0 Corp, their logo stamped on her blazer. Typically the goal was to make an android as close to human as possible, but this one's creators had no such goal in mind. The cut black suit she wore was form-fitting and tailored, and the proportions were all wrong for a human; her upper torso gave way to an unnaturally narrow midriff, thighs and calves bulky with clear muscular power. Her skin was porcelain white, with creases along the face and neck to allow for movement and speech. Her eyes were the real prize, though. They were black orbs with luminescent blue irises that glowed from deep within. She was composed with expert Japanese precision.

"You are Hiro Tarokata, correct?" the android asked. Her accent was vaguely oriental, like she had come from what was left of Osaka. Hiro confirmed his identity. "My name is Izanami. As you can see I've come on behalf of the 1Akuz0 Corporation. Have you been approached by any strangers tonight seeking shelter? I'm in pursuit of a very dangerous individual and I know she is in this approximate area of the Bloc."

"She must have done something pretty bad if they sent someone like you...Izanami-San, was it?" Hiro responded. Izanami nodded, and he noticed her eyes flicked restlessly between himself and the dojo behind him, scanning for something. *Or rather, someone.*

"Yes, she has. She's stolen some extremely valuable property from the Arcology near here, and contributed to the death of one of our enforcers. You haven't seen any strange children tonight, then?" she asked again.

"No. I haven't." Hiro said, definitively.

"I see. Very well then, I hope you have a good night, Tarokata-san." She bowed low, her body at an odd angle, and Hiro responded in kind. As she stood upright again she added, "You should know that if you do see our fugitive, any aid you lend to the company will be rewarded richly. It's not often that one with your record retires from 1Akuz0. Goodnight, Mister Tarokata."

With that, she turned and walked off into the city rain and neon lights. Hiro shut the door behind her and let Levy out of the cupboard she was crouched in.

"We need to have a talk," he said. He poured her a cup of the tea, while replacing his own with a fresh cup,

and the pair sat across from each other at a low table. "So-
"

"So, why is a murder bitch-bot chasing after me through Arc?" Levy cut him off. *For a young kid, she sure likes to be in control of the conversation*, Hiro observed.

"The 'Bitch-Bot' mentioned you stole something valuable. I have little patience for thieves."

"But human trafficking is just fine, huh?" she shot back. Hiro offered a questioning look which said, *Please, continue*. "What I stole," she used air-quotes, "were my own organs. I escaped from a body farm not far from here, in one of the Scrapers, 1Akuz0 H.Q." Hiro sipped from his tea, listening.

"See, I'm a universal donor; Type O Negative. This means my blood, spinal fluid, and organs are extremely valuable on the market. I was raised in that building to be drained and have all the pieces of me auctioned off like a pig at market! Well I didn't like that idea, and neither did..." As she trailed off, Levy seemed to be lost in thought and was less boisterous than before. Hiro let the silence stand until he had finished his tea.

"Neither did who?"

"A friend of mine. He told me about you, gave me your name."

"Where are you going?" Hiro asked after a brief moment of silence.

"It doesn't really matter, just out of the city. Thought I'd go for the Fringes, maybe." Her tea had stopped steaming a while ago. He doubted it was still warm.

"A girl your age, and as valuable as you are? Forget it, the Fringe would be suicide."

"So is staying here, or anywhere in the city after pissing off the 1Akuz0. They're the number-one company for security outsourcing, I don't know any place in the city they aren't patrolling," she said.

"I know they are. I used to work for them as an

Enforcer, or didn't you hear the android?" Hiro asked her quietly, but she did have a good point. It was the difference between absolutely getting caught and slaughtered, or the chance of survival. At least in the Fringe, there was still a chance.

"If you won't help me, I'm still going anyway. I'm telling you now, I won't go back there." Levy crossed her arms. She was still calling the shots, forcing the ultimatum: help her, or not?

Of course that had been decided when he tried to close the door on her, and could not.

"I'll take you to the Fringe." He took her cup, which had gone cold and untouched, to the sink. "We'll leave at 600 hours, during shift change. The streets will be most crowded then, and we can slip by without being noticed." Levy responded with a big smile and Hiro shot her a cold look, his grizzled face stern. "Let's make one thing clear. You need to do what I say, WHEN I say it. Understand? This won't be easy, and we probably won't even survive."

"Yeah totally, thank you so much, um...Tarokata...Senpai?" She struggled with the proper honorific. Hiro sighed in response.

"Hiro. Just call me Hiro."

***

They left at 6:00 on the dot, with hoods drawn up over their heads. The pair slipped into the crowd of hundreds, half made up of pedestrians moving into the factories and corporate HUBs for their twelve-hour shifts, and the other half ragged men and women leaving those same factories. The everyday lifeblood of Arc milled about them, and Hiro hoped it gave them the camouflage they required.

On top of a nearby building stood Izanami. With the eyes of a hawk, she saw man and child leave Hiro's dojo before dissolving into the current of people.

"Tarokata, I knew you wouldn't disappoint." She secured twin katanas to her shoulder harness, and raced off along the rooftops with a smile.

Not long after, Hiro and Levy were speeding towards the center of the city. Scrapers whipped past as Hiro wove in between cars on the superhighway, and overhead the homes of Arc's wealthiest floated through the air like clouds in the sky. When she realized their direction, Levy had some complaints.

"We're going the wrong way!" she shouted at one point in the stolen car. She produced a wakizashi, a short bladed katana, from her clothes, but Hiro grabbed it before it could be used on him. Snatching it just below the guard, he stabbed it into the car's expensive leather seat, just by his leg, out of her reach.

"I am not going the wrong way." he explained casually, and even though only one hand was on the steering wheel while he executed the maneuver, his eyes never once left the manic road ahead of him. "It's true; right now we're pointed towards the center of the city, BUT, and this is a pretty big but, there are no roads that go toward the Fringes; at least not major ones like this." Levy calmed slightly. Hiro continued.

"Obviously there are specific places that lead to the Fringe, those are the gates. The thing is, those gates are all on extremely small side streets and alleys. These are just regular city Blocs crammed up against the perimeter wall." Levy nodded while he explained. It made sense, since there was only so much room in the city. *You had to pump out the refuse somewhere.* "The quickest way to those alleys is to go right through the city along the autobahn. It'll spit us out relatively close to the wall, then we can make our way on foot." Hiro took a chance and spared a second-long glance at his co-pilot in the shotgun seat. "Sound good?"

She said it did. He gave her the blade back.

Even travelling at roughly a hundred and fifty kilometers an hour, they were still on the road all day, and only reached a stopping point as the sun began to set. Night falling in Arc was really something, and even Hiro stopped to watch as the transformation fell. The sun made its way lower past the horizon and as the shadow grew over the city, its touch ignited the brilliant light of neon billboards, buildings, and businesses transitioning to their night mode. The city came alive every night as darkness fell. Hiro always forgave himself this little bit of romanticism.

After night had fully fallen he took Levy by the hand and led her to a place they could lay low. The sign for "Caliban's Calibrated Cabaret & Suites" was particularly gaudy, made of halogen lights, with "& Suites" clearly added as an afterthought by a proprietor who wanted their business to have alliteration.

"Calibrated Cabaret?" Levy asked, pulling her hand from Hiro's for the fourth time. "What's this bullshit? It looks like someone strung Christmas lights on a house fire."

"Watch it, I can't protect you if your mouth picks a fight with every person in the city." The place was a sty though. The building was dilapidated brick, the color of which had long been washed away with rain. Garbage was piled up around it, with addled derelicts strewn amongst the trash which had been cleared just enough to free the door. "It's a Virtual Reality Suites. Shitty hotel rooms on the cheap. The only reason anybody uses them is because their tastes are too bizarre for conventional entertainment. As such, the employees don't ask too many questions."

The interior did not betray any expectations set by the exterior. There were couches lining the walls that were probably impressive when Hiro was a boy, but now were soiled and stained from decades of lounging. Guests were splayed out on the couches, most strapped into headsets, slack grins plastered on their faces and drool dribbling down their chins. Some had just passed out with needles in their arms. Hiro and Levy made their way to the desk where the concierge sat with an expectant smile.

"And what may I help you with today, sir?" He addressed Hiro with a salacious smirk and leer. His eyes slunk over to Levy briefly before snapping back to the older Japanese man. "I see we need a room for more than one, you dog, you. May I suggest a suite with communal Jack-In links?" He became more animated as he continued. "A wonderful bed with a shared virtual experience for a tawdry liaison. A private theater, perfect for menage à-" Hiro cut him off before the look in the concierge's eyes made him visibly ill.

"Just – whatever room you have, don't care about specifics. I don't need all the bells and whistles, it's not like that. She's my..." *Shit, we need a cover story.* "She's a corporate Server Monkey. Maintenance, you know. We won't be here long." The concierge looked at least slightly disappointed, but continued.

"Of course, sir. I didn't mean to assume any, um..." he cleared his throat and stood straight. "Well anyway, I have a fine room available, there is only the question of payment."

"There's a 2024 model Roadster I just drove into your garage, should be worth about...200,000? Anyway, it's yours now. I won't be needing it, and I forgot my wallet, so consider it collateral for the night." They signed a disclaimer that legitimized the bribe, and that was that.

The hallway leading up to their room was something of a nightmare, as well. Levy noticed a pair of guys huddled in a corner, shivering over some shared device in their hands. She couldn't see exactly what it was, but Hiro recognized the bloodshot eyes and manic grins on their faces. These were Cyber-Psychos through and through, and he nudged Levy over onto the other side of the corridor so he stood between them and her. He figured they probably weren't so far gone as to be completely berserk, but they could have been one, maybe two hits away from losing all rational thought. Better safe than sorry, so he pushed the girl into their hotel room and then crept in himself. He only took his eyes off the pair, who sized him up as well, to double bar the door with thick steel beams (security provided free of charge, of course).

"So what now?" Levy asked.

"Now we rest. I doubt the 1Akuz0 don't know you're with me, and I don't know how long we have. Hopefully a day, most likely less." He threw his bag onto the floor and propped his sword against the bed frame, collapsing onto the mattress fully clothed. It gave an unappealing groan as it sagged under his weight. "I'm going to sleep. I recommend you do the same."

"Yeah, sure." She paced around the room. Aside from the one bed, which was barely enough to fit Hiro, there was an armchair against a wall, framed by the light that bled in through the window that dominated the entire exterior wall. Levy drew the solid metal blinds down to eliminate most of the neon, and it triggered energy efficient light bars along the ceiling that radiated a dull orange light. "All in all, I'm disappointed but not surprised. Eh, Hiro? Hiro?" But he was already breathing deeply. "Right, sleep."

Hiro was asleep but far from resting. His dreams were always dominated by the worst memories from his long career as an Enforcer, but they were much worse tonight; more vivid because he had left the seclusion of his dojo and gone out into the world.

They started as they typically did, his earliest days as a fresh hire before even his first augmentation. He relived every kill and hunt he executed that awarded him another prosthetic. The 1Akuz0 loved him, and thought of him as a killing machine. Eventually, they used him exclusively for more sensitive work. He shuddered violently in the musty hotel bed as he relived the abductions. The bosses wanted virgins, young fresh meat for a new endeavor. Half of his body had been replaced by then, an unheard of honor bestowed on a lowly street rat the company had pulled from the gutter.

He dreamed of a beautiful woman with hair as black as the void, who trusted him completely to keep her safe. Another new venture, 1Akuz0 needed her alive and unharmed, so he kept it professional, and delivered. Still, he loved her, as much as he was allowed to. She smiled when they said goodbye. He smiled back.

"Dinner some time? There's a great noodle shop not far from here, open 24 hours." *Please say yes*, he thought.

"Sure, Hiro. I'll see when I have some free time." She never saw him again, but he saw her. Oh, he saw her. She hated the Farms, the entire Organ Donor project. She abducted several children and tried to get them out of the city. He found her alone in an alley, soaked through in rain and neon. She was radiant, like an angel trapped in this awful world by wings that were burned away. Higeki Amane never saw Hiro when he ran her through with his katana, and never saw the tears running from his eyes, washed away in the rain. The familiar vision haunted him:

Raven hair against the neon light. Cold steel warmed by fresh blood. Children's laughter, and children who would laugh no more. A lonely warrior, wizened by sin.

If he could save just one child now, like she had wanted to, then maybe he could start to forgive himself, he had thought. He had to believe it. Tears soaked his pillow, as there was no rain to make them disappear this time.

Hiro awoke hearing the bar on the door shut. Levy walked in with a cigarette hanging out of her mouth, long since smoldered down to the butt, and the empty pack crumpled in her hand. Hiro watched her stand for a minute in the dull orange glow. When she moved and stumbled as she made for the chair, he knew she was drunk. After Levy curled up in the armchair, he sat up and wiped the cold sweat off his brow and neck.

"How long was I asleep?" he asked

After a silence, Levy responded. "Dunno." Hiro

checked a clock glowing on the wall, and saw it was nearly 3 A.M.

"Well, how long were you gone?" Another silence.

"I dunno," she mumbled.

"Right." Hiro stood up out of bed and gave a stretch, wiping the tears from his face while his back was turned. "I suppose I need to tell you not to go wandering off every time I shut my eyes. What would have happened if you got picked up by one of those Cyber-Psychos in the hall, huh? I can't always protect you, you need to do some of the lifting here too!" He raised his voice as he laid into her.

"I'm sorry..." She slurred the apology and Hiro heard muffled sobs. He turned to see her sitting in the chair with her head in the crook of her arm, trembling as she tried to hide her tears. Hiro was all too familiar with trying to hide one's weakness, and it hurt him to see her like this. *God, she looks so small.*

Moving quickly, he knelt before her and took her arms to her sides, making her look him in the eyes. Levy was biting her lip, and tears had streamed down her face unnoticed when she first returned. Her shoulders shook with each breath.

"Hey, I'm sorry, I didn't mean it. Are you okay? Not hurt?" he looked over her neck and arms, free of injuries. But lifting her shirt to her belly button revealed a nasty bruise that covered most of her abdomen. "Levy, what happened? Who did this?"

"I'm sorry...I didn't want to cry." Her sentences broke and shook with her heaving shoulders. Hiro held her by the arms to keep her steady.

"Don't worry about that. Levy, who hurt you like this? I told you I was gonna keep you safe when we left, didn't I?" Her breathing steadied, but her head still swayed under the influence of alcohol.

"No, no, those are old. It was before I met you." She fumbled around, feeling for her pockets. "Where's my ci-cigarettes?"

"They're gone, how old are they?"

"They're just a part of growing up in the Arcology, it's old news..." She pulled her knees back up to her chin and looked past Hiro at the wall, but not seeing anything. "I haven't told you about it, have I? 1Akuz0 H.Q?" She blew air in a raspberry. "I wasn't exaggerating when I said it was like being raised to slaughter. I hated every second in that fucking place."

"Tell me about how you got out then."

"What difference does it make?" She demanded loudly, angrily. He could tell she was hurting though. *This facade; the smoking, the alcohol, the swearing, and brash behavior was hiding pain and guilt...and fear.*

"You'll feel better." Hiro said calmly, pulling a second chair and sitting across from his charge. "Besides, I'm awake now. There's no point going back to sleep."

"Feel better...fuck off..." Nevertheless, she continued. "It wasn't just me in there, at the Arcology, I mean. There was a couple dozen of us...kids." She slurred and rambled as she went on talking to Hiro, but each sentence came easier than the last as she finally opened up.

They were all children, the oldest might have been fourteen. She didn't know for sure because they weren't allowed to fraternize, instead being relegated to isolated rooms. The only consistent face to face interaction she had growing up was with an Enforcer inside who was assigned to make sure she stayed alive.

"Because suicides were really common if we were left unsupervised, you know," she said matter-of-factly. "His name was Zed. Maybe it might have been a code name, but he just said 'Call me Zed, what's your name'. He was really the only person who ever asked me my name."

She and Zed grew close, and while he'd developed a soft spot for all the kids they were keeping for the Body Farm, getting to know Levy personally was the straw that broke the camel's back.

"He grabs me one day, Hiro, and he says: How'd you like to feel the rain?" Levy sniffled in her chair, her voice had cracked from talking but Hiro wasn't going to stop her now. "So we go out into the hallway and he tells other guards we were going for a quality check, but he took me up the stairs and I could see the whole Bloc from those windows. He pulled me along and said I'd like the view a lot better outside. When we got to the roof, I-" she swallowed a sob before breathing steadily again. "Christ. I'd never been outside before. Can you imagine what that's like? I mean, I'm sure I must have, when I was a baby, but I don't remember anything then. I was thirteen years old when I tasted the air for the first time, and when I stepped out onto the roof, I collapsed."

"When you see the world from picture books and through an occasional window as you pass by...nothing can prepare you for how it feels, how it smells, Hiro. Arc smells like damp, and shit, and exhaust fumes, but I couldn't breathe deep enough to fill my lungs with it." She wiped her eyes, and Levy looked at Hiro without any barriers up for the first time since she arrived on his doorstep. "I love this city, Hiro. I'll never lose it or let them make me an animal again. Even if I have to go out to the Fringes, I'll have the lights at night and the smell of it in the air."

"Zed? He died, didn't he?" Hiro asked her softly.

"Yeah. He got caught up with that woman, the android who's been after me. He told me about you, some old guy who hates the 1Akuz0, then he made me run away without him. Said it was better to free others and die a man, rather than live with his shame." She relaxed her posture as she let out everything on her mind. "I think about that a lot."

Better to die a man than to live with your shame, huh? Hiro had never met this Zed when he was with the company, but he liked him. If only he had been that wise in the past. He picked Levy out of the chair, and moved her to the bed. He pulled the blanket up over her shoulders and sat down on the edge beside her.

"This Zed sounds like he was a smart man. A good man. If he was the one who sent you to me..." He paused, thinking of what he wanted to say. "Then I'm glad he did, Levy." Resolve strengthened within him, like steel in his gut. "I won't let them take you. I promise." Hiro spent the rest of the night sleeping in the chair while Levy snored silently and the beat of rain played on the window.

A few hours later, Hiro had woken Levy and the pair had cleaned themselves up to leave. The night had passed without any soldiers breaking down the door, so Hiro was cautiously optimistic about their chances for a successful escape. The hallways were void of guests as they made their way to the lobby, taking every corner slowly. When they at last came to the lobby, Hiro poked his head around the corner.

"It's dark, I can't really see anything," he said, squinting but unable to make anything out clearly. "We're just gonna go for it, stay close, and-"

"If anybody calls out just keep walking, got it." Levy interrupted. Hiro had to suppress a laugh, *this damn kid*, he thought. They were halfway across the lobby when the lights flicked on, and revealed the grisly scene. Bodies were stacked up on the couches that lined the walls, their throats slit and covered in blood. The concierge from the night before was similarly dispatched, slouched over the desk with Izanami leaned across it nonchalantly.

"Levy, get behind me and stay back," Hiro commanded Levy, his eyes fixed on the approaching machine. His sword was out and raised before he finished the sentence.

"I gave you the chance to turn her over, Tarokata. If you refuse now I will kill you." He remained silent, so Izanami charged.

She was incredibly fast too, her mechanical legs helping her glide across the floor to meet Hiro, who was already in a defensive position. He brought his left arm up and blocked the opening strike with his own prosthetic, metal ringing like a clear bell. Immediately on impact, he pivoted his right hand and brought his sword up under her arm to strike at her midsection, which she predicted, blocking with one of her two weapons. Her hand had literally rotated at the wrist-joint to guard against his attack, and she smiled as she triggered a quick burst of voltage through her hands, up the blades, and shocking Hiro to lock up his muscles briefly. With one leg, she kicked the stunned warrior across the lobby and back against the empty hotel bar.

"You know I could have killed you just now, fool. Give me the girl and you get to live. I'll only take your prosthesis as punishment." She slunk up to him, where he was leaning against the bar top. "You can still earn forgiveness."

"There's only one way to earn my forgiveness and it won't be at the hands of your masters," he said, and brought a hefty glass bottle crashing against Izanami's head, causing her to stagger back as the glass exploded in her face. "I guess human or otherwise, a whiskey bottle makes a pretty heavy strike." Hiro dove in for a deadly thrust, but his blade was knocked wide by another rotation of Izanami's arm. She had her own sword below to slice up under his arm and into his chest, which would kill him instantly, and he was wide open.

"Not as good as you might think." Her blades were rising now, adrenaline slowing it down to a painful crawl. *Things are funny like that when you're about to die*, Hiro thought.

Suddenly the blade stopped dead in its tracks, and Hiro looked up to see Levy had dropped a VR headset onto Izanami's head. Her whole body was frozen at once as her motor skills redirected from her limbs and into the virtual space. He could see her fighting against it, small movements and twitches where the android was wrestling control from the headset, so they didn't have long. Levy ran for the door and Hiro pushed Izanami onto her back and, using his mechanical arm for added strength, impaled her with her own katanas. They stuck out of her abdomen, blades buried all the way to the hilt. Even if it didn't kill her, it would take precious minutes to pull them out, and they could use that to make their escape. He sheathed his own sword and chased Levy out the door.

"Wipe that smile of your face and fucking run, we aren't that far from the wall." He took her by the hand in the foggy daylight, and they sprinted down the maze of alleyways to put distance between themselves and the rapidly recovering killer in the hotel lobby.

* * *

It was actually something of an exaggeration when Hiro said they were close. After running for nearly an hour in a vaguely easterly direction, the last half of which he had to carry Levy, he finally let them stop and took a seat to catch his own breath. They didn't stop for long, and continued heading east through the alleys at a much more relaxed pace than before.

In claustrophobic corridors such as these, the massive billboards and LED displays were replaced with a different type of advertisement: old-fashioned shouting. Every hole in the wall belonged to a bar, restaurant, or vendor, and they all strained for business. The smells of synthetic meat frying on a stove on one corner mixed with a man shouting about his strip club just around the next one. There were billions of businesses running in Arc, and they all wanted a slice of the pie.

Hiro pointed Levy towards one of the ramen carts as they broke out into a small street with several dozen people milling about. They had reached their destination at last, and he wanted to stop so they could have a bite to eat.

"Who could turn away such a beautiful young girl?" asked the old lady who owned the ramen cart. They sat with their two cups of fried noodles with egg substitute (who could afford real eggs outside of the Arcologies?) while Hiro eyed the gate that sat not more than two hundred meters away. Levy asked why they didn't just go for it now.

"We're scouting the situation first, to see if the gate is being watched by more than its typical guard. Besides, there aren't any places outside the wall where we can get a meal like this just whenever we want." He took a deep drink of the broth.

"We?" Levy asked, looking up at Hiro.

"Yeah, 'we'. I'm staying in the Fringe with you. I told you it would be suicide out there by yourself, and besides, it's not like I can go back home. I'll be just as dead as you if the Corps catch me." Hiro held up his metal arm and knocked it against his legs, also prosthetic. "Only they'd take all this back, so there would probably be less of a body." He smiled at her.

"Was...was that a joke? From you?"

"Yeah."

"Your first joke in two days is about being a mutilated corpse?" She laughed so hard she had to put her dish down on the counter and take a moment to recover herself. "Christ Hiro, you're just as fucked up as I am!" They both laughed a little too loudly, considering they were trying not to draw undue attention, and ordered a second bowl each to celebrate their successful escape. The ramen woman gave them both a scowl and grudgingly obliged.

Might have celebrated too soon, Hiro thought as they were stopped on the way to the gate.

"That's far enough, Tarokata." A man's voice came over the air as the sound of the people around them suddenly stopped. Hiro and Levy had paused in the middle of the narrow street that the alley afforded them. Looking around every one of the people who had been going about their business, at least over a hundred of them, had stopped and turned to face the two runaways.

"Fuck." Levy cursed under her breath. The man spoke again, this time stepping from under a shadowed doorway and into the drizzle that had started.

"I'm sure I don't have to tell you that we have you surrounded, but well..." the man looked around, "We have you surrounded." He was 1Akuz0. A man in his early forties, old Japanese descent, with a shock of red hair slicked back in the rain. He wore a long black coat that reached to his knees with an expensive shirt he kept unbuttoned. Hiro recognized Takeshi Kira, President of the 1Akuz0 Corporation's Security Force. Hiro began to pull his katana out slowly. "Ah ah ah, not so fast. I think you know better than to try something like that against your old boss, eh?"

"Are you here to stop me?" Hiro called out across the distance between them. "Here to demand the girl yourself, and promise me clemency if I surrender?" He looked around, and even the old woman who made their food had a rifle aimed at them now.

"Nah, nothing like that, I'm just here to kill you." The bluntness was a refreshing change of pace. "We'll probably kill little Levy here too, but that's not my call to make. She really pissed off the top brass."

"How'd she do that? By robbing you of one more child to auction off to Arc's wealthiest?" Hiro called back. If he could keep them talking, maybe he could find a way out, even if he could just save Levy. If he was fast enough.

"It's not about the money, Hiro, you know that." Takeshi answered, not moving any closer. "It's the principal of the thing! One girl runs away, what next? More kids run, that's what!" From the corner of his eye, Hiro saw Levy distancing himself slowly. *Good, now I'll just keep their eyes on me.* Raindrops grew in size and turned the drizzle into a full shower.

"Like when an Enforcer retires, eh? What did you say to me back then, Kira?" Hiro shouted, commanding attention over the sound of the water.

"Nobody leaves this life. Least of all people like

us." Kira replied. "And you said 'Watch me', so watch this, Hiro!" He flicked his wrist once at his side and Hiro turned to see one of the plainclothes men grab Levy by the wrist, using a prosthetic hand that fired off like a grappling gun. It clamped around Levy's upper arm and dragged her towards the soldier across the damp street. All Hiro heard was a loud "NO", followed by Takeshi barking orders at his Enforcers.

"Shit somebody grab the girl, she's got a knife, PROTECT THE FUCKING MERCHANDISE!!"

But before Hiro, Takeshi, or any of the Enforcers could make a move, Levy produced the wakizashi and plunged it into her stomach, crying out and falling to her knees. Even with his enhanced speed, Hiro couldn't move fast enough. While he dashed the short distance between them, Levy gritted her teeth and pulled the blade horizontally across her belly before twisting it, and yanking it upwards into her heart. The harakiri had slashed through all the organs that 1Akuz0 considered so valuable, and Levy looked at Hiro with a triumphant smile on her face, and something akin to relief in her eyes. The soldier released his grip and her arms fell to her sides. She collapsed in the street, her blood mixing with the rainwater around her in a growing viscous pool.

Hiro lifted her small body from the water, ignoring the viscera on his clothes. He couldn't hear anything over his own heartbeat and the rain, which was now coming down in a torrential downpour, but he spoke to her there in the street. He apologized for failing, for his history with the 1Akuz0, and for her ever having to experience this kind of life. He looked up, and for a second could see Higeki standing over him. She frowned a mournful frown and disappeared, leaving only Takeshi and Izanami, who had arrived to stand alongside her employer. The two spoke, and she began to walk into the flooded street. Hiro rose to meet her, and the two stood face to face without their weapons drawn.

"I asked that I be the one to execute you, because I wanted to prove myself after our fight in the hotel." Izanami said, her robotic features glistening as the water slid off of her.

"She was my only chance for forgiveness. I don't care how I die now, as long as it's a warrior's death. You or anyone else will get the job done, Kikai," he said coldly.

"You call me 'Machine'? Tarokata-san, you misunderstand me. I was as human as you or Takeshi. Or Levy, I suppose," she said, sparing the girl a passing glance. She drew her weapons and stepped two paces back, falling into a defensive stance. Hiro stepped back as well, drawing his single blade and holding it aloft over his head, poised for attack.

"No," he said defiantly. "Levy was more human than any of us. This company wanted to make me a monster, a weapon used for wanton slaughter and fear. NO LONGER." Izanami nodded, but was otherwise unfazed.

"You probably don't even remember me, but I joined the Enforcers when you were still the most famous soldier in the Corps. I looked up to you. Hell, we all did, Hiro. And when you left, turned your back on us?" she laughed wryly. "That was my chance to be just like you. I did everything they asked me to, killed who they wanted, and eventually, I surpassed you." They paced in circles while she talked, never taking their eyes off of each other. "By now, the only human part of me left is my brain. I've become the ultimate killing machine."

"So?"

"So you were the one thing I never got to face. You're my last test, Hiro Tarokata. Now fight me, and I'll give you the release you crave!" They leaped at each other through the rain, clashing with metal swords and limbs striking each other until the ringing was one uninterrupted sound.

The katanas arced through the rain with neon light reflected off their blades, glancing up the length of

Hiro's arm, or Izanami's legs as she somersaulted into a follow-up attack. Hiro was getting hit. She cut him on his chest before pivoting around, and striking again from behind. She was faster than him in every way. He could block however he wanted, but she was there waiting, already midway through her next strike. She refused to fatally wound him though, instead cutting his arms, or slashing a red wound across his chest. His clothes were in tatters as she proved her superiority with a wolfish smile juxtaposed against her mechanical features. When their dance ran its course, and they finally stopped moving, it was only because Hiro had been stabbed through his abdomen from behind.

Hiro held the blade in place with his mechanical hand, protruding from his stomach, keeping Izanami from pulling it out. She moved to strike with her off-hand blade, aiming at his neck, and he pivoted and snapped the blade in half while it still skewered him. Izanami's second sword collided with the ground after the clean miss and Hiro kicked with the manic strength he had in those legs he had earned from the 1Akuz0, destroying that weapon as well. Finally, in his free hand he took Izanami by the neck and threw her into the flooded street, pinning her with the full weight of his body. Just like in the hotel, he impaled her through her chest, opening vital electronics. The rain water pooled into her wounds, seeping inside and shorting out every manufactured limb and organ she had relied on for so long. The resulting shock fried her brain, and she lay dead in the street.

Takeshi and all his Enforcers waited to see what Hiro would do next as he knelt hunched over the dead 'Android'. He stood up slowly, looking to the sky. Night had fallen, and Arc had come alive with a million neon lights. It made rainbows of every single raindrop as they crashed on Hiro's face, now devoid of tears. He turned to Takeshi and started walking, only to be shot from behind in the shoulder. He continued, pulling Izanami's splintered blade from his body, blood washing out in the rain. It was already over.

Takeshi screamed some order that Hiro couldn't hear, but there was the sudden thunder of gunfire from all directions. He felt some bounce off his prosthetic limbs, but most sunk into his flesh. He broke into a sprint with one thing in mind: *Kill Takeshi Kira. Earn your death.*

Next thing Hiro knew, he was on his back in the watery streets, watching the lights play on the sky. He was cold, but it wasn't bad. It felt more like coming in from a summer day, and the rain was just a cold shower to wash away the sweat. He lifted both arms to the sky to catch the rain. They were both human.

GETTING CLEAN

By Max McCamish.

In stale air, the cognitive function of the human brain goes down by ten to fifteen percent. The carbon dioxide in the air is what does it. Every time Dr. Amy Kandry touches down back in the concrete trench near Arc's city walls, her breathing feels more labored, her thoughts more fuzzy; at least half of it is simply knowing how polluted the air is. It's easier to breathe in and around the towers, and again, half of that is simply knowing how clean it is there.

Amy's legs are braced with the mechanical upgrades she'd obtained when she was a lot younger, dated but high-quality cybernetics designed for parkour that she'd kept up herself throughout the years. Her biological legs are weak at the knees, but the thin, twisted metal around her legs allows her to land gracefully from twenty-foot-long jumps without the pressure of normal human limitations, espe-cially the limitations of a fifty-year-old woman with slowly encroaching arthritis. She drops easily from the rooftops onto the dingy gray streets of her neighborhood, affectionately called 'the pit'. The thick air is unpleasant, but the colorful lights make it feel just that little bit less bleak, even though a regular resident easily grows numb to them.

Towers of concrete go up either side, blocking out the natural light of the moon. There's a general smell of several individually unidentifiable things, that together smell salty and earthen, even though there's no earth to be found. It's late, and the asphalt is still wet from the rain, but the street is not empty. A few of the unfortunate majority huddle in doorways, tattered coats over old clothes, and some of the slightly-more-fortunate hurry past, hoping not to be bothered on their way home. Bright advertisements burn the weak eyes of the pit's residents, blue and red and white light clamoring for attention, noises and flashing colors that cry out to be noticed. In a sea of attention-grabbing things, nothing stands out.

Amy slickly joins the foot traffic on the ground level, squinting into the darkness between neon lights to find what she's looking for. Her own home is a concrete hole in the wall, hidden in a nook between corporate buildings with eleven other dwellings, all studio apartments that barely fit even that much. Coming from wealth, Amy almost could've complained about her situation. Of course she misses living in the towers, but she has no choice in these matters. Ever since she lost her job at Walker Global and had to dive fully into the criminal underside of the city, this has been her life, and it isn't as bad as it could be.

She locates the familiar clothing advertisement that's dancing and gesturing enticingly. She slides in behind the billboard, into the tiny passage that only the sharpest of pedestrians would notice, and along to number five. Tapping the screen on her wrist and flicking along it twice opens her key, and holding her wrist to the door causes the iron to slide upwards into the concrete. It's near the outer walls, and it's tiny, but at least it's secure.

She clambers up inside, and when the door senses she's passed through, it shuts again. The roof is not much higher than Amy's head, and the room is wide enough to fit just a single mattress, a small fridge and a camp stove, a few shelves full of precious books and presents from her children, and boxes full of her tools and collection of parts. The backpack that Amy wearily drops on the ground clunks on the concrete; those items are to join the collection.

When she was a little more lawful, Dr. Kandry had been a recognizable name in the field of cybernetics. Her research had helped to develop new ways of hacking the brain and enhancing the intertwinement of human and machine. Of course, when she was caught stealing cybernetic parts from Walker Global and selling them for personal gain on the black market, and was subsequently fired, the praise around her name fell a little. Which, in the end, may have been a blessing in disguise; the over-infusion of cybernetics and biology has been blamed in some publications for the rise in cyber-drug usage. Amy's once coworkers and peers are being put under fire by a significant number of news outlets with sizable audiences, and while Amy would forever rather be inside the walls of the towers again, she's at least grateful to not have that on her plate.

Now, instead of selling the parts for a profit, she fixes them. The black-market cybernetics are almost always of horrifying quality. The difference from Walker Global to the clunky, fritzy machinery she works with on a daily basis is night and day. Wherever most merchants are sourcing their cybernetics, it isn't from anyone like her. The poor souls who purchase these enhancements almost always end up worse for wear, and they come to Amy for a hope in making things better. For a fee, Amy replaces the frayed wires, rewrites the botched code, strengthens the fragile joints, and makes the artificial muscles move the way they should. It's the only way she can think of to apply the skills she'd gained in the research and creation of these things, and it works for her. It's what she'd spent her whole life doing, aside from her brief flirtation with professional sports in her teenage years. Oh, those years were a long time behind her. How pleasantly innocent those years were.

"Home, do I have any messages?" Amy's voice activates a white plastic unit on her bookshelf that lights up at the sound. For a moment, the light spins in a little circle as the machine reads through its memory, before pausing.

"One message." The machine has the voice of a pleasant, yet tired woman. Officially, its name is Tomi, but that's the name of Amy's eldest son, and she can't bear to call his name every day when she can only see him once every few months. So, she'd renamed it, uncreatively, 'Home'. "The sender is: Mel. Would you like to listen?"

Amy only saw her children every few months because she'd left them with her sister, Mel, inside the towers' walls. With how she was living, it was best for them, and she didn't regret it—although it tore at her heart sometimes. "Yes. Please." Anything Mel had to say was important to Amy, more important than anything else. If it was news on her children, good or bad...

Mel's voice, a little distant but easily recognizable, came through the machine. *"Hey Amy, I meant to call under better circumstances, but it's Micah. He's... well, we think he got a dose of bad juice, maybe, it's... hard to tell what's going on with him. He's in a bad way. Tomi's doing what he can, and I'd call a doctor if I could, but I really can't afford it, and I'm thinking—I know you're a doctor of cybernetics, not a medical doctor, but juice, it's at least partially cyber, right? And you know some medicine. You've got to be able to do something... or, at least, the kids want you here. Can you come? I'll get you through the walls, don't worry. Come to the north-east gate as fast as you can, and I'll meet you there."*

As soon as the message clicks off, Amy has her wrist to the door lock, opening it again. She'd been looking forward to dinner, but dinner is forgotten as soon as her children get involved. Micah is sixteen, a year younger than Tomi, and seven years older than Amy's only daughter, Avalon. He's far too young to be getting into any sort of drugs, but he's a kid whose curiosity is never satisfied, and his emotions are easily messed with. He hasn't been doing well ever since Amy had to leave him behind, and she knows this, but she hasn't thought for even a moment that he could be doing something as drastic as juice to get by. Tomi had told Amy of his suspicions, but Micah had denied it.

Oh, Amy's as mad as she is worried. She's seen what happened to those who abused the drug. Cyber-psychotics, some called them. It's not a strictly medical term, but with the cultural connotations of the word 'psychotic', it's easy to see where it's come from; the grins of people that saw the city as their playground, the citizens as toys to be played with, broken, and tossed aside. Forgone from reality in favor of euphoric delusions of grandeur that are easily dangerous.

No son of hers will ever be lost to the world like that.

It's at times like this that Amy's machine legs show their true potential. As soon as she's out into the street, she bounds with the full force of her upgrades and springs ten feet up into the air, clearing the building and flying through the smoke emitting from the vent below. She coughs through it, her weakening lungs still robust enough to recover quickly, and makes headway into the darkness. Neon lights guide her path through the air, using buildings as her landing pads to push for thirty more feet of distance. Like sprinting, but each step crosses a building and reaches a height that would break her legs on impact if it weren't for her upgrades.

When she reaches the limits of the middle-class boundaries, it becomes just a little more difficult. The wall extends up into the smoggy night sky, too high for her to jump and too smooth to climb. The street below is busier, even at this time of night, people bustling back and forth about their somewhat shady night business. The sounds of vehicles whir above, although their shapes can't be made out in the grey sky. There's a walkway, not far to Amy's left, that connects to the north-east gate above. The only traffic across it is a few weary workers returning home to the pit. Nobody is entering.

Amy changes that. She leaps, with the full height her cyber legs can reach, and soars through the air to a graceful landing on the edge of the walkway. The lights along the path illuminate her as she runs uphill, the gate coming into view quickly. The guard, a big man in 1Akuz0 uniform, is deep in discussion with a cloaked woman, whose voice Amy recognizes immediately.

When she arrives, she sidles up to the conversation, gaining context before attempting to join in. "...just coming back from work," Mel says, completely calm in her act. "Her authorization system was malfunctioning recently, and we haven't had time to go get it fixed yet, so she asked me to—oh! There she is!"

Even though Mel's face is fully metal on the left side, she's remarkably expressive. The guard turns to meet Amy's eye, sizing her up, comparing her and Mel. "Your authorization system is glitching, yes?"

"It is. I am so sorry, we've been meaning to get it replaced." Amy is not as good of a liar as Mel is, and the urgency to get to Micah's side is encouraging her to rush through the interaction. "I've just been busy."

"What is your work?" he asks. Both of his arms are reinforced with cybernetics; he's not someone you want to pick a fight with. Mel looks at Amy, a silent nod communicating to her that she needed to come up with this lie herself. Amy turns around and takes a brief glance at the road beneath her, the hustling back and forth. What could they be doing? Black market sales, drug deals, red light work, maybe. A few people are at food stalls, others peddling upgrades to electronic body systems. Everything she can see, or think of, is illegal or far to lowly skilled for a middle-class resident to be out here doing. Amy quickly realizes she doesn't have a good lie. So, she tells something that twists the truth just enough.

"I work in cybernetics. I fix them. There's more work out here." Not a lie; just misleading. The guard's dark eyes take in every detail of her face, and she notices a tinge of unnatural blue light in his iris. A scanner. Looking for signs of a lie.

He catches none; only signs of urgency. "Alright, I'll let you through, but only this once. Get your software fixed before going outside these walls again."

"Thank you so much!" Mel grins, and when the glass slides open to let Amy through, the sisters run to meet, on Mel's side of the glass. "We've got to hurry, but thank you, sir, it won't happen again."

They take off at a hurried pace, Amy slowing herself down to match Mel's natural speed. The pavement here is newer, harder and more even. There are fewer broken windows, fewer people huddled in doorways, fewer dim alleyways. There's more advertisement around them, and it stings Amy's biological eyes. Both of Mel's eyes are mechanical, and she has no such issue. She had to get her left replaced after an accident shot a piece of metal into her skull, but she soon replaced her right when she experienced the improvement technology had over what her human body had grown.

"How are we getting into the tower?" Amy asks. Her sister is taller, thinner, and more agile than she is naturally. Mel is fast, for someone who's never cybernetically altered their legs. They're making good pace towards the center of the city. "That won't work twice, and definitely not to get into the towers."

"Don't worry. I've got my back way," Mel says, winking at her. "Mind you, someone still has to get us in, but this time we won't have to lie. I'd tell you, but you'd flip."

Amy narrows her eyes suspiciously. Mel's face is outlined by the neon lights, and her exact expression is hard to make out in the darkness, but the mischief in her eyes is clear. "I will not. I must know."

Mel laughs. "I'll let Tomi tell you."

Amy rolls her eyes; unlike Mel, she can't forget the situation at hand quite so easily. She's never been able to shrug off the weight of the world and laugh in the same way as her sister. When her son is in trouble, in pain, she can't question what secrets her other son might be holding from her. She goes along with Mel's jokes, but can't feel it.

Their run doesn't take as long as Amy had thought it might. They twist through the streets, the shopfronts and homes getting progressively nicer, bigger and more open as they come closer to the center. It's not the towers, not yet, but it's a hell of a lot nicer than where Amy lives. In this part of Arc, not one person is out on the streets, excepting one patrol that eyes the party of two, but asks no questions. Amy counts her blessings on that front.

Mel leads her around the impressive wall that loops around the towers, stopping at a camouflaged door recessed into the wall, a tiny red light the only thing indicating that something might be here, until one finds the seam. Mel runs her finger along the wall until she catches both sides of the door and knocks squarely in the middle exactly four times. Amy watches, catching her breath as she waits, until there's a clicking sound inside the wall, and the metal begins to shift sideways, opening up into a small chamber lined with concrete. A teenage boy, nineteen at most, stands there, nervously running shaking hands through his thick black curls. The first thing Amy notices about him is the lack of immediately identifiable cybernetics.

"Quick," he says, and Amy wastes no time in hurrying into the small chamber, Mel right behind. The door silently shuts behind them, and the kid holds his finger up to a pad on the wall that scans his fingerprint before allowing them all access. "You guys should be able to get in pretty clearly from here. I'll follow up behind. It's, uh, nice to meet you, Ms. Kandry."

His nerves reflected what many people felt when they met Amy for the first time. "It's Dr. Kandry, actually," she says, a stern brow raised at him. The boy lowers his head and quietly apologizes, but as soon as the door opens, Amy runs ahead. She used to live here; she knows the towers, and doesn't need help to find Mel's home.

Despite living inside the towers, Mel is not highly ranked at Walker Global, in comparison with where their parents, and indeed Amy, used to be. Her home is only the second floor up, and that's easily reachable by one jump, for Amy. Her children know this; the window into Mel's apartment has been left open. She knows the tower well enough to be certain it's Mel's.

"I'll see you inside," Amy nods to her sister. Mel and the boy head off towards the door, while Amy runs to the window and jumps, before anyone could see her and ask any questions. She catches the edge of the metal window-sill with her hands, pulling herself up with more effort than she thought it would take, and drags herself into Mel's living room.

The lights are dimmed, and Amy quickly realizes it's for Micah. She spots him immediately, lying on the old red couch and twitching, his eyes flickering wildly around the room as though asleep, but with his eyelids wide open. He's sweating thickly, and the screen on his wrist is showing an error code.

"Oh, my baby," Amy whispers under her breath, running to his side. She takes notice of everyone else in the room secondarily. Tomi is sitting by Micah's side, and Avalon is sitting a little further away, holding a pillow to her chest. Mel's only child, Jay, stands in the doorway with a worried expression, as silent as ever. Micah seems completely unaware of his siblings, his cousin, his mother.

Amy springs into action. "Tell me everything you know," she instructs Tomi, taking Micah's wrist and reading the error code. *Unable to connect to nervous system.*

"Well, he's not been coping well, you know that." Tomi's voice shakes slightly, but he's putting on a brave face so as not to scare the others. His mother can't be fooled by it. "There's no use pretending. He's been doing things off the street. Shootups, viruses, a few harmless things, but lately, he's done juice a few times. Only a few, he's not a cysyc or anything, but I've been trying to tell him... doesn't matter. We think he was told it was juice, but they've given him something else. Because this isn't juice, right?"

"No, it's not," Amy concurs. "Or if it is, there's something seriously wrong. Whatever he's on seems to work both on the cybernetic level, and on the nervous level, which juice does. Your nervous system is, generally speaking, supposed to interface with your cybernetics, which is what makes juice possible in the first place."

She takes a small selection of tools out from a pocket in her pants, tools she hadn't had a chance to unpack from her scavenging trip. The tiniest of them is a long, thin piece of metal that hooks under a corner of the screen in Micah's wrist and flips it open, exposing the parts underneath. "Ideally I'd be able to check the connection between his chip and his brain directly to see what's going on, but that would require surgery. I'd wait until it's one of our last options."

A quiet whisper comes from just behind Amy. Avalon's words are uttered so softly into the air that her mother almost doesn't hear them. "Is he going to die?"

"No." While Amy is about eighty percent confident that that's the truth, that still means she's twenty percent lying. She doesn't yet know what this drug can do, or how similar it is to drugs she knows. She's not even sure if it's just contaminated juice, or something else entirely. She doesn't often lie or stretch the truth, and that's why it's so easy for Avalon to believe her.

Amy begins to take apart the plates to reach the biological flesh underneath, where the cybernetics connect.

"Are you going to take him with you?" Avalon asks. It breaks into Amy's concentration, and she tries her best to not let her annoyance show.

"No. He doesn't have to go." When Amy had left, it had been very hard to explain to Avalon why she'd had to go without them. Without knowing what Mel had told her, Amy thinks it best to leave it vague. She isn't particularly keen on explaining that she was a thief.

Avalon nods and stays silent, leaving Amy to her work. With the wires that lead into his nerves exposed, Amy can see that they are, in fact, connected and working—and that the error message itself was incorrect. Feeling the wires with her fingers, they're burning hot. They're not disconnected, but going into overdrive.

She begins to shut the metal panels again as she considers this information. A nervous stimulant; this was echoed in the sweat on his brow, the twitching of his fingers, the rapid movements of his eyes. An overdose, perhaps?

This is a case in which Micah might, and that is a might, be very lucky, simply due to how unlucky he had been.

Micah has limited cybernetic enhancements; he has the same screen as the rest of the family, and the same neurochip as everyone, but he also has an artificial organ attached to his spine at the base of his neck. When he was younger, just like his aunt and his grandmother, he'd had a twisted spine. In his case, it was fifty degrees of scoliosis that had to be corrected to twenty with metal rods nailed into his back. At that time, they'd added the unit at the top of his spine, so that slight adjustments to the length of the rods could be made, and to add −or remove− medication that was normally injected into the spine for pain relief. While it isn't what the unit is for, it does have the ability to cleanse the spinal column of foreign substances. If it works for medicine, it might work for whatever this is.

It's worth a try, so Amy shuts the metal panel in her

son's arm. "Tomi, come help me sit him up," she instructs her eldest son, and, with apprehension on his face, he comes to his brother's side and helps to lift him. Amy can tell something is bothering him; behind them, the door opens and shuts again. Amy doesn't have to look to know it's Mel.

When Tomi is distracted, sharing a look with the boy from before who anxiously slinks into a corner, Amy knows it's time to ask. "Okay, out with it," she says as they get Micah leaning up against the back of the couch. He twitches slightly, his eyes rolling over to fix on his mother's. His mouth moves, but makes no sound, and Amy can't lipread. She wants to think he recognized her, that he's at least that aware.

"What? Oh." Tomi realises she's talking to him after a moment. He catches the boy's eye, gently gesturing for him to come closer. He's reluctant to do so. Amy moves Micah gently, shuffling in behind him and lifting his shirt up to read the metal panel in his back. Tomi helps support his weight, keeping him in that position. "Yeah. Mama, uh, this is Gray, and, uh..."

Amy doesn't look up at either of them, her focus on finding the corner to open the panel with. "Go on. Make it good news."

Tomi's nerves tell her that isn't the case, but she hopes anyway. Maybe he's just nervous to introduce a friend, or more than a friend. That would be fine.

"...and we're going to go over the wall." At those words, Amy fumbles the tool she's holding and nearly loses it. A small curse comes through her lips without her permission, and it takes her a moment to fully understand his meaning.

"Do not tell me you mean to leave the city." It makes sense when Amy looks at Gray; he has no cybernetics, a trait shared only by those too poor to afford them and those who consciously reject them. He lives in the towers, so it can only be the latter. He doesn't look like Amy's typical idea of a luddite; but then again, she's never met one before. She had never expected her son to become one. "You will die."

"No, I won't," Tomi protests immediately. Amy quickly remembers the situation at hand and returns to opening up Micah's back, although she still has an ear for her elder son. "It's not like how they tell you it is out there. It definitely can't be any worse than where you live, except there's no chip in your brain that can be used to track you down and hack you and there's no chance of *this* happening." He nods towards Micah at 'this', and Amy feels a visceral reaction rise in her throat.

"Where I live is terrible." Her normally steady hands feel less steady as she reveals the panel and finds the button she's looking for. One press, and it should begin to detox any foreign substance in Micah's spinal fluid. Whether or not it'll work for the drug he took is uncertain still, but it can't hurt. "You do not want to give up your place here for that. This happening is not the fault of the city somehow. Micah did this to himself."

"But clearly—clearly he's miserable here. Why else would he have done this?" Tomi protests, a gentle hand on his mother's shoulder. She's tempted to shake him off, but doesn't do it. "I'm miserable too, Mama. So's Avalon. We all want to be with you more than we want to be here, and if we leave, we can all be free together."

"Free from what?" Amy snaps back. A small drop of clear fluid comes from a hole in the metal plate of Micah's back, and Amy wipes it away. That's good news, at least. "Free from luxury? Ease? Opportunity?"

Tomi is silent, expecting a longer rant from his mother, but it's interrupted by a hacking cough deep in her lungs. The smoggy air she jumps through every day takes a toll on her, even when she's clear of it. "Like this. The air is clean here. Out in the fringes, it kills my lungs. Do you want that?"

Gray speaks, in a move that is clearly brave for him,

as he stumbles into the sentences clumsily, like a foal learning to walk. "I—the pollution is created by the city. Because nobody here cares about clean energy, or what's best for the people on the outside. The people above us, they care about themselves, and that's all."

"And why do you think leaving will make that better?" Amy has the argument in her head, but in her heart, all she really cares about is making sure Micah is okay. He's twitching less, and the clear liquid is coming out a little bit faster now. Amy hopes to any supernatural power that might exist that her idea is working. "Everyone outside only cares about themselves, too."

"Don't you feel empty?" Gray asks, and that gets Amy's attention. She stares him down, and while her intense gaze does cause him to falter, he doesn't fall entirely. "It's—being here, in this place, it feels like nothing is natural, and it's all fake. I think everyone is kind of disillusioned with that."

"How old and primitive does something have to be to be natural, I ask? Can we have no modern conveniences? Must we be cavemen?" Amy is not so much mad as cynical. Whatever Gray wants to do is none of her business, but her son is going to stay where he is safest and best cared for. "Nothing is ever truly good, or perfect. We give up some of the natural for our ease. You live so much better here in this tower than you ever would anywhere else. Don't be deceived that it's otherwise."

She turns her attention back to Micah. The fluid is beginning to build up faster, red-tinged with blood. Amy's hand sits on his shoulder, and he reaches for it, shaking fingers gripping onto his mother's.

"And," she adds into the stunned silence that follows her words, "...modern technology might be saving your brother."

The room is on edge. Micah makes a sound somewhere between a groan and a word, but nobody can understand what he might've been trying to say. Amy rubs her fingers over his, hoping to give him some semblance of comfort in whatever pain he's in. With the drug affecting his nervous system, he might be numb, or he might be in unimaginable pain. His relative silence was reassuring.

"Mama," Tomi says, a soft, furtive word, checking the air. Amy twitches slightly at the sound; everything about this situation is stressful. She doesn't want to lose Micah, and equally so, she doesn't want to lose Tomi. If he leaves the city, she likely won't see him again.

She sighs. "Yes?"

"I don't know about me, or Avalon, but I think it's best for *Micah* if he's with you."

The impact of his words strikes harder as Micah grips at Amy's hand. Amy bites her lip and finally looks over at Tomi, considering. His eyes are wide and honest, begging almost.

Amy is not one to bend on her ideas. She wipes some of the fluid away; she hasn't been able to hold any of her children close in a long time. She's seen them on occasion, but never for long, since she had to move out of the tower. She certainly wants to live with her kids again, but she doesn't want to put them through the life she lives, and certainly, this is better?

"I'm not so sure," she argues, but it's weaker than her usual definitiveness. Her family all recognize this as a sign of her budging, and it piques interest.

"I agree that he isn't doing well," says Mel, walking over from the door. "I don't think being around you will necessarily fix it, but it'll make a difference, surely. It started when you left."

"He hasn't been holding down any kind of work I've tried to help him get," Tomi explains, beginning to strike the thick end of the wedge into his mother's resistance. "There's a cybersmith that Mel is friends with, and we managed to get him an apprenticeship with her, but he wouldn't go. He hardly leaves his room, and when he does, it's to cause trouble. He never wants to talk to anyone. He wasn't like this before."

"No, he certainly wasn't," Amy agrees indignantly. "You haven't just been allowing him to do these kinds of things, have you, Mel?"

"Of course not," she says, scoffing at the very idea. The sound of a drone flying close overhead drowns her out for a moment, and she restarts her sentence. "He's acting strange, not because he doesn't respect me, but because he's unhappy. I see this all the time in my patients. People come to me, rich and successful beyond their wildest dreams, powerful, famous, enhanced, and yet, the wonder why they aren't happy. They're lonely. Human connection is the best predictor of happiness."

"You're all his family as much as I am," Amy contests, looking around the room at her family. "Mel, you think this is a good idea?"

Mel shrugs. "You're his mother. And if I'm behind it, well, that depends." She turns to Gray, raising an eyebrow at him—the eyebrow on her flesh side. "Hey, kid. What's your plan for leaving Arc? Where would you suggest we go?"

"Oh, uh, well." Gray's still nervous as all hell, trying not to shake. The attention of the entire room is on him. "We can go pretty much anywhere north, or west. Or south, I guess. Up north, there's a lot of land that's still green. People live on it, in rural villages. They have enough technology to easily grow food, and there's a lot of work that can still be done there. And yeah, there's not a lot of technology—you can't just go to a cyber technician and get wings installed— but... can any of us do that any-way?"

"We could," Amy says. "Once."

Gray nods quickly, taking a moment to realize she wasn't arguing. "Yeah, well, it's. I, personally, think it's a lot better than living here—I mean, if you want to hear what I think—"

"Just speak," Amy urges with a grit of her teeth. Micah's leaning on her, and when she tilts his head to look at his eyes, they're closed now. Not madly flitting like they were before. It brings a warmth to her chest that's been missing for a while.

"Well, I think there's something beautiful in being human. Technology is fine, it's great, but it should supplement our humanity, not replace it." His words still sound idiotic and somewhat luddite to Amy; there's a completely separate appeal to the idea that Tomi encompasses perfectly.

"I don't care about that, so much as getting our family back together." He places a gentle hand on Avalon's shoulder. "Life here is only good and viable if you can afford it. And if you can't, Mama, then I don't want life here."

"Avalon?" Amy asks, raising the question to her only daughter. Avalon rocks back on her knees, biting her lip in uncertainty.

After a quiet moment, she says, "...will it mean Micah stops hurting himself? And you'll come back and live with us?"

Tomi answers, not Amy. "Yes, it will."

"Then that's what I want," Avalon agrees easily, "but Aunt Mel and Jay should come with us too."

Amy sets her jaw. "I'm not sure I like the idea of just uprooting and leaving Arc like this. Is it really so bad? You can all have any material things you want here. At least, you will be able to if you get a job and work up the ladder. Tomi, it would be so easy for you. Why don't you want it?"

"Because you can't be a part of it." The genuine pain in his voice strikes Amy, tells her how much her children care for her, and there's a pain in that, somehow. It's a pain in knowing she'll have to leave them. Or worse, that she won't, and she'll drag them into a far worse life because of it.

And Amy turns to Mel, hoping she would knock some sense into her children. Mel gives her a long shrug. "Look,

I'm happy enough here. But Jay's father left the city, and he never came back. Which means he's either dead or happier. So, that could be a vote for, or against." Mel laughs at her own dark joke. "No, but seriously. If we're going to go, we should go. Kid, uh—what's your name?"

Tomi rolls his eyes where Mel can't see. "His name is Gray, Auntie."

"Gray, alright, dumb name but fine," Mel grins. Micah's leaning on Amy's shoulder now, and she cradles his head against her, so utterly grateful for her luck in dealing with this. She checks his wrist—the error code is no longer showing. "Credits are useless outside Arc, right? We can't use them anywhere else?"

"That is correct," he says. Amy doesn't miss that his hand is gently sitting on Tomi's shoulder. She narrows her eyes at him and he quickly moves it.

"So, we should go all out. Empty our bank accounts. I'll buy a plane or something that we can live in. Get everyone any cybers they want before we go. I have a lot of money sitting around, you know? I support four kids, after all. Amy, I know you're the sensible one and not me—"

"Damn right," Amy mutters, chewing on the inside of her mouth.

"—but surely you can see that this isn't that bad of an idea. We'll find the green land, Micah won't be able to go around getting high anymore, and he won't miss you anymore. You won't have to steal things to survive. You're a surgeon as well as a cyber technician, so you can do that. You'll be with your kids again."

"There's one person we haven't asked," Amy says, a last line of defense to stay. She turns to the ever-silent Jay and raises her eyebrow.

Jay almost never speaks, as a simple preference. But in this moment, Jay walks up to Mel and interlocks fingers with her, a sign to everyone else of agreement.

Amy is the last conscious person in the room to object to leaving. Looking at her situation, she has two choices—

and one of them is risky, stupid, and irreversible. It's the option that would make everyone happier. The other choice is something she can't take. Her kids' misery has become too much, and it's clear in Micah's current state.

"Fine," Amy sighs, like this has been a long and laborious decision. "We can go, as soon as Micah gets better. We must make concrete plans, however, and I have questions. My first question is for you, young man," she says, pointing a finger at Gray.

He nervously shrinks in on himself. "Y-yes?"

"Are you coming with us? You'd be leaving your family behind." She's already hazarded a guess at the nature of his and Tomi's relationship, but considering the talk they'd just had of family, it's important to make sure they weren't about to separate him from his own.

"I don't exactly have any," he answers, the tiniest of shrugs. "I don't really want to get into it. I want to come because... well, it may be a bad time to explain this, but I—"

"Yes, yes, I get it, you're with Tomi." Her condescending tone takes Gray aback, and a red flush spreads across his face. "Romance is dumb and stupid. It's why I had my kids all on my own. I advised Tomi against ever dating, but I suppose he's old enough to make his own decisions." Despite talking about him in third person, she looks at Tomi when she speaks.

Tomi blushes too, looking at the ground instead of facing his mother. In the silence, Amy presents her second question. "Gray, have you ever left?"

He pauses. "Briefly, yes. I didn't go far, a few hours' trip by plane, but I got a very good idea of what it's like. That's part of why I want to go."

That was encouraging, at least. They weren't going entirely blind. She can feel a cough beginning deep in her lungs, and the feeling is so tiring.

"And...what's the air like out there?" She asks, allowing the true softness of her voice to show for a moment.

"Clean?"

He has just the slightest smile on his face. "Clean."

LAYERS [TAYLOR WILL MESS YOU UP AND EAT YOUR SOUL]

By Tracy Cross.

"**D**o you have a problem?" Taylor York poked her long, brown finger into the man's chest. Even though he stood a good half a foot above her, she wasn't afraid.

She had a job to do.

"Did you not hear me?" She poked his chest, each word accented by each poke.

The man was all leather and beard. Half of his skull

was covered in silver-plating with blue cords climbing out of jack points. He looked down at her, his right eye focused on her face, "No."

"I suggest you leave or I will throw you out." Taylor moved closer, out of his line of sight.

He laughed. His friends surrounded her and laughed until she made a fist and punched him with an uppercut straight up, beneath his chin. Her cybernetic arm made her four times as strong. She knocked him off his feet and onto the table behind him.

"I see we have come to an understanding. Now leave."

The man's friends scrambled over to the table and lifted him. They draped his arms over their shoulders and dragged him across the pulsing dance floor. No one missed a beat as Taylor made her way back to the stool, next to the bar.

"Was all that really necessary?" Ai, the bartender, asked as he poured her a glass of water.

"Is it ever? They see me and think I'm not…you know. But nowadays, I have to keep my arm super oiled and loose." Taylor grabbed the glass with her human right hand and tossed back the water, "More."

"Sure, Taylor. As long as you protect me when I leave." He joked as he poured more water in the glass.

Someone at the other end of the bar waved. Ai nodded his head in the direction as Taylor refocused her attention to the huge dance floor.

They didn't make discotheques like this anymore. Lights shining above down onto the floor filled with people moving like worker ants, one way then the next. Bodies covered in sweat writhing against each other in an alleged sexual frenzy. Actual deejays that played actual vinyl records and old school mixes. Tonight's deejay was "Lady Kitty" and she loved music from the 1990's.

"Taking you back with a 'French Kiss'!" Lady Kitty yelled before she let the needle drop.

Arms flew into the air as bodies swayed. The electronic beat was hypnotizing as Taylor tapped her foot at the bar. Ai motioned to her to join him on the floor. She shook her head and smiled, "No thanks."

Decker, another bouncer, walked over and sat next to her, "How can you listen to this absolute crap every night?!"

"Not every night! I'm only here on Friday, Saturday and Sunday. I work 'Bio-Tatts' during the week." Taylor turned towards him, "How late you staying tonight?"

"You tell me, boss." Decker slapped a huge hand on her shoulder. It felt like a clamp gripping her as she shook him off.

"We are just about at last call, why don't you do a sweep and you and the guys can go. Cool?" Taylor slipped out of his grip.

Decker nodded and raised his meat hook arm towards the other bouncers in the club. Taylor watched them congregate, summoned by Decker. Then, they fanned out to different parts of the club to take care of whatever needed to be taken care of.

Taylor watched from the bar and smiled. She never questioned her luck—being a high school dropout and orphan—and she took everything in stride. It could all change in a moment. Best to be grateful. She watched Decker escort some burly guys out the door as the music continued.

Good riddance.

Lady Kitty and her black enhanced ears gyrated onstage. She pulled one or two of the other audience members up and danced in between. Someone yelled, "Kitty Sandwich!" They gyrated onstage as their bodies meshed together-sweat on sweat, flesh on flesh until Lady Kitty touched an earpiece.

"Time to wrap it up, Kitty. Security has to clear the place out." Mai, one of the supervisors spoke.

"Acknowledged," Lady Kitty said.

She slipped towards her deejay stand and grabbed a microphone, "I wanna thank everyone for coming out tonight! We gotta wrap this up! I'll see you beautiful depraved souls tomorrow!"

Someone flashed the discotheque lights before slowly turning them up. The crowd began to disperse. Taylor walked up a set of stairs behind the bar that led to the control room governed by Ai's sister, Mai. Taylor pushed open the door and walked in. Mai's hands skillfully worked across keyboards, adjusting cameras as she stared at the screens.

"What do we have, Mai?" Taylor asked.

"Taylor, good to see you. Nothing suspicious tonight. Got some 'Beta Girl' recruiters outside. I told Tadin to go break it up."

"Good deal," Taylor walked up behind Mai and watched the monitors, "I just don't get the whole 'Beta Girl' thing. Why try to recruit outside a nightclub? Especially this shithole, which is in the worst part of the 'Lowers'?"

"Hey, they aren't looking for real girls or 'Alpha Girls', so I wouldn't worry about it. I mean the best a 'Beta' can be is at least half synthetic." Mai whipped around in her chair, "I mean, that is why I gave them up. They are addictive but eventually, you just get tired of them."

"Too much, Mai. You are just too much." Taylor smiled and laid her hand on her shoulder.

Mai whipped back around to the screens, her arms moving across the screens and knobs like porcelain spiders. Her jet-black bob hit the top of her spine, which was enhanced with a chrome metallic covering beneath blue lights and a jack point at the top.

"I'm going back down to wait for this mess to clear out. Let me know if there's trouble outside, Mai. I'm leaving soon."

"Taylor, you taking Ai home?" Mai tossed out.

Taylor paused, "Actually, I was going for the deejay,

but if she's not, I guess I can settle for your brother."

Taylor saw Mai's face fall, "Unless you wanted the deejay."

Mai chuckled and waved her hand, "Good night."

Taylor watched the cleaning crew push brooms, mops and garbage cans on the dance floor. Ai finished cleaning the bar and the guys finished their sweep outside. She thanked everyone and started walking towards the employee exit.

Ai ran up beside her, "You and me, tonight?"

"Maybe we should cool it. Your sister is acting all weird again." Taylor slipped on a heavy black leather jacket. She rotated her right arm in a circle, listening to the clicking of metal on metal.

"Meh, whatever. You shouldn't worry about her. I can make you feel good." Ai pulled his jet black hair out of the rubber band. It cascaded onto his shoulders. He shook it out and smiled at Taylor.

"You see, this!" She stopped walking and pointed at him. "This is all unfair. Working it like in the old days, huh? I'll bet you drove them all crazy." Taylor led the way down a short greenish-tinted hall towards a black door.

She pushed the door open and the smell of the city and the night air filled her lungs. This place always smelled like desperation and sadness. Maybe if she lived in the better sky apartments, things would smell better, the air would be clearer and it would not taste like she was sucking the exhaust of one of the few city buses. Ai followed her out onto the dock. He lit a cigarette as she sat and then jumped to the ground. They waved to the cleaning crew and walked down the well-lit alley and out to the street. Taylor stopped before they reached the edge and glanced around the corner. She saw a petite person, all in white, fall to the ground. A few men stood around the person and tried to hold them down.

"You will pay us! Took six of our 'Betas' last week. That ain't cheap! Boss said she didn't want trouble, but I don't mind." The leader turned and looked at the other guys, "Do we mind?"

The other guys laughed as the person on the ground tried to push away from the group. The leader reached down and lifted the person in the air. The person's feet slipped out of a pair of white stilettos. They clattered to the ground.

"They are picking on a chick?!" Taylor unzipped the zipper on her right sleeve. She rolled the jacket back far enough for a small circular device to pop up in her palm, triggering a device on her arm. Her arm glowed red as she took aim.

"Taylor, wait!" Ai grabbed her shoulder.

They watched as the small woman grabbed the hands of the man holding her in the air. She managed to pull her legs beneath her before she unleashed a string of kicks to his face. He dropped her and she swept her leg around, close to the ground, knocking all the men over. She popped up and jumped on the leader's chest. He reached up but she snatched his hand and bent it backwards until it couldn't bend. She ripped it out of the socket and crushed it.

"I don't know who you think I am, but people like you don't touch me! Do you understand?" She growled as she leaned close into his face.

"You need to hear this." Taylor listened to the headphone Ai gave her. She listened through the enhanced earbud and softly, beneath the woman's talking, was the sound of something savage and low. An animalistic sound. A growling.

"I scanned her. She's not hybrid. She doesn't have enhancements..." Ai began.

"But she has very good hearing." The woman in white turned and looked straight at Ai and Taylor in the alley, "Let me finish this up, please."

For a moment, when the woman looked at Taylor, Taylor felt her stomach drop. Her mouth started to water and a feeling swept over her that she hadn't felt in a long time. A very long time. A hunger gnawed at her stomach. It was so strong, she put her hand on her stomach and leaned forward.

"Shit!" Taylor groaned. "What is this?"

"Just one more second." The woman spoke as though she were stacking papers on a table or taking out the trash as she decimated the gang. A white Toyota Futari whipped around and screeched to a halt next to the woman in white. The door raised. A very apologetic man jumped out and scrambled on the sidewalk. His legs moved like jelly as he was followed by three more silent men.

"I'm sorry. I'm sorry."

The woman, with an astounding casualness, turned and looked at the men. "Fernando. Fernando...Fernando...how many times..."

"I'm sorry, Miss. *Por mi vida, lo siento*." He fell to his knees and bowed low.

"I warned you and your boys. Fernando, I gave you a chance, right? I mean, you are in the business of protection and yet, I'm not feeling protected." She spoke as the men moved the bodies somewhere Taylor and Ai could not see. There was a small sound and a bright white flash.

Taylor and Ai turned away. When they looked back, the woman had on black wraparounds and stood in her extremely high stilettos. Fernando lay on the ground. The back of his head looked like a balloon full of red pasta sauce had exploded as he mumbled, "I'm sorry, I'm sorry..." until his life pack died and the light in his eyes dissipated.

"Get this piece of shit out of here before..." The woman pointed to the remaining men as the police pulled up.

One of the officers stepped off the holobike and started to step towards the woman. A second officer grabbed his arm and mumbled something. The first officer nodded and they disappeared as fast as they appeared.

Taylor passed the earpiece back to Ai and strutted over to meet this woman. This woman with the power to kill on the street and send cops away. One word popped into her head: power.

"I need to be a part of your life," Taylor thought as she left Ai behind.

"Taylor York. I know you. It's kismet we were in the same area tonight. I was going to come observe...again." The woman lifted her wraparounds and extended her hand.

"And you are?" Taylor extended her hand.

"Names are not important." The woman shooed her away.

"Well, I needed to know what I should call you when I roll over and get you coffee in the morning."

Ai appeared at her side, "Or at least when we all grab a bite later...at my place."

The woman smiled. Her high cheekbones, dark eyes and equally dark hair was almost hypnotic, "Catori. Catori Bly."

"Catori—interesting name." Taylor shook her hand and held for a bit longer than she should, "Are you 'Native'?"

"My parents were 'Native'. I'm just me and I like a well-educated woman and her..." Catori raised an eyebrow as she smiled at Taylor. She glanced at Ai, "Is he your lover?"

"I'm open." Taylor glanced over at Ai, "I mean, we are open. You know. *Open.*" Caught up in the woman's beauty, Taylor felt something inside her glitch. It was like she didn't have control over her own body or brain.

All the nerve endings in her body, those that were truly hers, were on fire.

"I'm a collector of information. We should discuss this after we get some sleep?" Catori motioned for them to get into the car, "The three of us? I mean, if everyone is okay with...sleeping."

This woman's power reached out and pulled Taylor towards her. Taylor wanted to walk over and kiss her, suck her soul from her body.

"Taylor, let's go." Ai nudged her and broke her concentration.

"Thanks, I needed that. Where are we going?" Taylor slid into the soft white leather seats.

"Up. Have you ever had champagne and watched the sunrise?" Catori's voice wrapped itself around the car and Taylor as the car doors closed.

Taylor furrowed her eyebrows and glanced at Ai. Even he seemed to be under Catori's spell. He reached down and grabbed Taylor's hand, almost as though trying to send her a telepathic message.

"No worries, my lovelies. It's going to be a beautiful night. Buckle up." Catori smiled and pressed a few buttons. The car drove itself and in the next few moments, everything on the ground shrank as the air became clearer.

Catori filed her fingernails as the car began to ascend. It was very smooth and subtle. If Taylor and Ai didn't glance out the window, they would not have known the car was moving. Ai reached down and grabbed Taylor's thigh. Taylor stared out the window in amazement.

Taylor never went into the "Uppers" before. She noted how the buildings were black and covered with soot at the bottom. The further up they went, the cleaner things seemed. Even the night air seemed cleaner and clearer.

"Look at this," Catori leaned forward and pointed out the window. "Bruno, hover."

"I didn't know cars were equipped with 'Bruno' units. I thought they were just for..." Ai began and stopped when he followed Catori's finger.

The sky was a dark blue and the stars twinkled. Neither Taylor nor Ai had ever been this high up in a hover car. Taylor sharply inhaled as she whipped her head around and she tried to take everything in. Everything seemed to hover: buildings, casinos and cars. There was a police officer directing traffic.

"It's a whole different world up here." Taylor was amazed but kept her responses flat.

"My place is over there...beyond the pale blue square right there."

"What is the square?"

"Our green space and mall." Catori sat back in her seat.

"What's the point in having green space in the air when you can have it on the ground?" Ai quizzed as he sat back in his seat. "I mean everything is better on the ground."

"The only thing life down there holds for me is information. I collect it, like I said. Who wants to hang out with 'Beta Girls'? Even those punks in the alley were disgusting. Once you've had a life up here, you never want to go back."

"And yet, we found you down there, slumming with us." Taylor smirked.

"I came looking for you, Taylor. I need *you* in my life."

An officer with a jet pack tapped on the window. "Will you need an escort?"

"No, we are fine. Just wave us in, Frank." Catori pressed a button and her voice was outside the car.

The officer waved them into the apartment.

***

Taylor crawled out of the huge bed and slipped on a thin white robe covered with Japanese characters. She looked back at Ai, sound asleep, his hair fanned out on the pillow.

She stepped out of the room and closed the door. She followed her nose to the smell of actual food being cooked. She was amazed with the size of the apartment—high ceilings, huge windows and enormous fluffy sofas. Catori stood in the modern but minimalist kitchen weaving her hands over pans as Taylor walked over to the breakfast bar behind her.

"So, how do you know me? I mean, we didn't clarify any of that last night." Taylor rubbed her shoulder, beneath her cyber arm.

"Didn't seem to matter." Catori's hands busily moved over pans on a huge stove. She moved so fast, it looked as though she had two sets of arms.

Taylor saw a cup on the counter and grabbed it. She glanced back at Catori. Catori motioned towards a basket next to the coffee maker. Taylor grabbed an espresso tab and dropped it into the coffee maker. She slipped the cup beneath it as the coffee brewed. "Well, I put my intentions out there."

"And I accepted them. None of this is important right now, let's eat. Do you eat traditional or tablets?" Catori wore a long, single braid down her back and it swung like a pendulum when she moved. She also wore a pair of black silk pajamas, giving her the impression of gliding around the kitchen.

"Where are the plates?" Taylor asked. "Should we wake Ai?"

Catori pointed to a cabinet near Taylor, "Not until after you and I speak." Catori placed a pan on the island, a distance from Taylor, "I need you. I collect information. I want you to come work for me."

"I'm a bouncer. I work in a tattoo shop on my off days. How would I qualify to collect information? Especially for an 'I Broker'?"

"I think you know." Catori raised an eyebrow.

"No, I don't." Taylor sipped the coffee.

Catori continued cooking.

"I don't do that anymore. Thank you for the night." Taylor placed the empty coffee mug on the counter, "And, I've lost my appetite."

"Didn't think you had much of one." Catori smirked.

Taylor reached for the mug and gripped it with her

cyber hand as she grit her teeth, "What did you say?"

"Like I said, I collect information. I just want you to work for me and maybe gather some info here and there. I'll make it worth your while." Catori walked over and adjusted Taylor's robe.

"I. Said. No." Taylor felt her jaw clench.

"I'm sure I could help change your mind." Catori leaned in and started to kiss Taylor on the lips as she opened her robe.

"Can I get in on this sandwich?" Ai walked in the room wearing a towel wrapped around his waist. His shoulder length, damp hair was pulled into a sloppy ponytail.

"I was leaving. Do what you want." Taylor pushed away from Catori and held her robe closed as she ran towards the bedroom.

"You hungry?" Catori joked as she placed a strawberry in Ai's mouth.

"Always." Ai grabbed Catori by the waist and pulled her close to him as she bit part of the strawberry in his mouth.

Taylor walked into the bedroom and found her clothes on the floor. She began to dress as Catori wandered in and watched from the doorway.

"Who knew you had all those curves under there? Such chocolate deliciousness." Catori purred.

"Is that all you wanted?" Taylor pulled her shirt over her head and fixed her spiky black hair.

"You saw Fernando. I need new security. You don't have to get information, how about we try out security? I need someone that truly has my best interest at heart. I even have a separate suite here for you to stay. I will need you near me all the time."

"To protect and serve?"

Catori nodded and smiled, "Never mix business with pleasure. I'll pay you more than you make now. And if the situation arises...maybe you can get information from someone for me the old-fashioned way. You know, with your fists."

"I'd enjoy that very much. Using my fists, I mean."

"Great and…"

"I'll take a few days to think it over and I'll get back to you. Can you have a car take me home?" Taylor sat on the edge of the bed and slipped on her work boots.

"Sure."

"I'll be in touch." Taylor sat up and sighed after she tied her boots, "So, you calling that car or what?"

Ai stood in the doorway with a bowl of fruit, "You should really get in on this. It's better than what we eat down there. I could get used to this."

Catori smiled, eased by him and out of the room.

"What, you wanna be kept or something? You wanna be a 'kept man'? Ai, you just don't have the get up to be 'on call'," Taylor joked.

"If I lived up here, I wouldn't have any 'on call' problems." Ai sat on the bed next to Taylor, "Last night…are we gonna talk about it?"

"Nothing to talk about. Not like we are mutually exclusive, you know? I mean you are better than a 'Beta' anyday." Taylor leaned over and kissed Ai on the lips, "See you later or you know…next time I see you."

Ai reached up and caressed Taylor's face. He ran his thumb over her cheek and pulled back as she kept her eyes closed. He opened his mouth to speak but she leaned in and pressed her lips on his, again.

"Let's just leave it like this." She flicked her tongue on his strawberry-flavored lips. "Sweet."

"Car's here." Catori interrupted, "Or are we having a repeat performance?"

Taylor walked out the bedroom door.

***

As she was returned to the dank Lowers, she recalled being

a half-naked teenager in the kitchen with her parents. She wore a bra and panties as her father worked frantically over a boy laying on his back on the floor. Her mother yelled at her and pointed to the boy on the floor. Taylor felt tears stream down her cheeks.

"You did this! How many times, Taylor?! How many more times?!" Her mother yelled.

"I don't know if I can bring him back. He's barely got a pulse." Her father continued with chest compressions.

"What did you do?! How long was it, Taylor? Did we not warn you? Did we not tell you about doing this?" Her mother moved closer and pushed Taylor towards the sink.

"So what if I did do it. Maybe I wanted to!" Taylor wiped at her huge, brown eyes, "Maybe, maybe I *meant* to do it!"

"It was too much. I can't save him." Taylor's dad wiped his hands and stood. He leered at Taylor, "You did this. We should make you take care of it."

Taylor ran over and kneeled next to the boy on the floor. She put her fingers on his throat and felt for a pulse. It was faint, but the throb was there. She glanced back at her parents—her mother's arms crossed on her chest, her father's vacant stare filled her with dread.

"He's alive."

"If he is, it's your turn to fix it. We've cleaned up enough of your messes." Her father muttered, "If you can do it…"

Her mother reached an arm in front of him and silenced him, "She goes, regardless."

Taylor's lip trembled. Her vision blurred with tears as she pounded on his chest with a fist until he inhaled and sat up straight. His eyes bolted open and he stared at Taylor and scratched at his head.

"What happened? Where did your folks come from? What were we doing?" He wore a pair of black boxers and nothing more. He struggled to sit up. His body looked like a mass of jelly.

She didn't remember his name as she rushed around and picked up his clothes.

"Uh...you gotta go. I'll see you at school tomorrow, okay?"

He tried to stand again, and her father walked over and put his hand on the boy's shoulder, "Son, just take it easy."

The boy sat on the floor and held his head in his hands, "I-I-don't understand. Whu...whu happened?"

"You'll be alright, son. Give it a minute." Taylor's father glared at her as she deposited the clothes at the boy's feet.

A few minutes later, he dressed himself and looked at Taylor, "See you around?"

"Yeah, something like that." She muttered as he stumbled toward the door. Her father walked over and offered the boy assistance.

He stumbled down the long hallway as her father held him up. The boy glanced back at her, his eyes filled with a mixture of fear and nervousness.

"Get dressed and get out. We warned you." Her mother pointed at the door, "We told you and we tried to help and we covered for you. We *warned* you."

Taylor sat on the floor in her panties and bra. She looked at her bare feet and sighed. She knew her mother was right. She was warned and she knew the consequences if she was caught again.

"Well...well...I know you guys are the same as me. It would have been nice if someone said something before...like advice." Taylor stammered.

"Just leave, Taylor. Please."

* * *

Taylor went about her business as she considered Catori's offer. She was a dying breed of information extractor. There were not many of her type of extractors left in the world. She didn't know where her parents disappeared to, and she never bothered to look for them, after they kicked her out for what she did to the boy.

She was also perplexed as to how Catori knew about her. She left her old life behind. After her parents kicked her out, she went about forgetting who she was and most of her old life. She tried to eat food, but couldn't, because of her condition. She tried to live a normal life, as normal as a high-school dropout could afford. She was ousted to the Lowers, a part of the city where life was built around survival, as opposed to just living and loving life.

When she lived on the street and hustled for work, she hardly used her "skills" because she did not understand them. After hustling for awhile, she found a place to stay. It was further south in the city, where the rains seemed constant and the humidity was stifling. She moved into a walk-up squat. It was a partially run-down building that housed other runaways.

She managed to secure work and started working towards her high school diploma. For the first time she felt at ease in her life, until the day someone stole her stuff while she was at work in a tattoo shop, sweeping the floors, making appointments and cleaning out the booths. She felt good as she strutted home. When she stepped into her space, everything of hers not bolted to the floor, despite having a storage locker, was gone.

"Who took my shit?!" She stormed around and yelled as her jet black mohawk flopped. Her black boots were unlaced, her jeans were a size too big and they hung off her hips, and she wore a black hoodie that was two sizes too big.

"Huh?"

"My shit was right here! Mark! Mark! I paid you to watch my shit! Who came in and took it?!" Taylor stormed across the room to a teen sitting in a beat-up armchair.

"Whu?" His eyes rolled around as she yanked his head back. His hair was curly and slick with oil. His green eyes were unfocused and she wanted to punch each freckle off his face, "Ma?"

"I swear to. . . are you high? Are you fucking high right now?! Mark!" She yelled in his ear until someone came up behind her and grabbed her arm.

She whipped around and blindly punched someone in the face. The someone was Mark's stoner girlfriend, Mary. Mary fell back and sat on the ground for a moment. Taylor could not help herself and was on top of her, punching and clawing at her face, before either of them knew it.

"You fucking junkies sold my shit! You sold my shit!" She yelled as Mary laughed and spat blood out onto the dingy carpet.

"It was good shit too, you stupid girl." Mary growled.

Taylor pulled back and everything slowed down. She looked down at Mary's face, a bloody, pulpy mess, and smiled. Something raged inside of her, something so strong that Taylor could hardly resist. She leaned over and pressed her lips to Mary's, making a seal. She inhaled and felt it. She felt the life leave Mary and fill her soul.

She saw all Mary's memories and thoughts. She saw Mary and Mark getting high and making a deal to sell her stuff. Mary's entire day and subsequent life flashed through Taylor's mind in reverse. As the memories poured in, Taylor felt full. She felt her soul and spirit fill themselves until she managed to push herself away from Mary's shriveled body on the floor.

"Dude, looks like you went too far," someone whispered in her ear. "That chick is dead."

"Yeah, what's wrong with you? Why did you do that?" Random voices asked what seemed like a million questions.

"Is she dead? What did you do?"

And the inevitable word popped out of someone's mouth as Taylor stumbled to her feet, "Freak!"

They all chanted in unison, "Freak! Freak!"

A wave of embarrassment and shame swept over Taylor. She looked down at the body as her head filled with information from the memories; Mary's real name, her birthdate, the names of her parents. Taylor began spewing the information under her breath as Mark slipped beneath her and grabbed Mary's body.

"Freak! Freak!" The house chanted.

Taylor stood in a drunken stupor. The room spun as the information continued to flood her head. She ran her hands through her hair as she frowned.

"FREAK!"

She stumbled out of the room and out of the squat, never to return.

***

Having mulled over her life, she decided to work for Catori temporarily. She promised herself she would not use her skill, no matter how many times she was asked. After a few months of working for Catori, Taylor felt relaxed. She stood outside a door and looked down a long hallway.

"So far, so good." Taylor mumbled to herself.

The building was a very rich building. Everything in the hall screamed money and opulence. The carpet was tan with dark brown swirls. Every few feet was a table with fresh flowers. The hall was warmly lit, unlike the harsh fluorescent lights where she had lived. Even if she lived in a broom closet in this building, her life would have been infinite times better than before.

Taylor took her position outside the door as Catori walked inside. Catori paused. "Get rid of anyone trying to come inside, I've got work."

"Yes, boss."

"By any means necessary, understand?"

"Yes, boss." Taylor replied.

After some time, the door opened.

Taylor heard mumbled voices and the sound of thumps. For such a literally small person, Catori had a lot of power. She threw men around like ragdolls. Taylor wondered if Catori was part synth.

Minutes later, the door flew open.

"All done." Catori walked out and wiped her hands on a handkerchief. Then, she wiped her mouth and passed the handkerchief to Taylor.

"Did you get what you needed, boss?" Taylor quizzed.

"More or less. We can go." Catori breezed by her and walked down the hall.

There was a ringing and the elevator doors opened. Taylor pushed Catori to the side and reached for her holstered gun. An old woman pushed a laundry cart out and stared at both of them.

"Are you okay?" the old woman croaked.

"Fine, thanks ma'am." Taylor helped Catori up as they moved into the elevator.

"Well, you ladies be safe."

"Mm." Taylor nodded.

"What was that?" Catori snapped as the doors shut.

"You want me to keep you safe or you want some crazy woman to jump out and stab you or something? We gotta switch up these techniques." Taylor stood in front of Catori as the elevator descended. "Where next?"

"I've been working this guy over since before we met, and I just can't get the info from him I need. I hear there's something about high rises…"

"I'm sorry. What do you do with the information you get?" Taylor interrupted. "I'm curious."

"Well, I sell it. I use it to make my other business ventures thrive," Catori casually responded.

"Well, that can't be legal."

"Do you think anything down here is legal? Come on." Catori stepped close to Taylor and kissed the back of her neck. "Speaking of ventures, what say we get a couple of 'Alpha Babes' and have some fun tonight?"

Taylor closed her eyes, "Sorry, not interested. I was

hoping to run an errand after we were done. I have plans."

"Anything I can help with?" Catori wrapped her arms around Taylor and pulled her back.

"Not on duty, ma'am. Never know who's watching." Taylor pulled Catori's hands off her waist.

"I always get what I want. Never forget it, Taylor." The doors dinged open. "I got you, didn't I?"

"Maybe it was the other way around." Taylor walked out the building and held the door open for Catori.

Catori smiled as the valet pulled the car up to the building.

* * *

"Time for some stress relief," Taylor raised her arm and dialed Ai on her flesh colored gauntlet. A hologram of him appeared above her wrist.

"Was wondering if you were gonna call me soon, or if you were too busy with work." She watched as he ran his fingers through his hair.

"Whatcha doing tonight? I know it's your off night." She leaned back in her bed as she "tossed" the projection to a projection cube.

"You coming down to the 'Lowers' to see me? Or do you want me to come up there?" He was in bed and let the sheet fall to his waist, as he sat up.

Only Ai knew Taylor lived with Catori in one of the fancier, new sky apartments. Taylor liked the clean air and the space. Even though she had a single room, there was more space than she needed.

"I suppose I could come slum." Taylor leaned over the edge of the bed and looked for a pair of jeans. "Say in a few hours? At the discotheque?"

"Maybe you should just come to my place, you know I've got what you want." He cleared his throat. "What you need, baby."

Taylor rolled her eyes and sighed loudly, "I think a

'Beta' would give me more satisfaction. Look, I'll see you down there."

She terminated the call as she slipped into a pair of blue jeans.

"Going out?" Catori knocked on the open door before she slipped inside the room.

"My time is still my own, yes?" Taylor continued to dress. She dialed for a taxi on her gauntlet.

"I could drive you."

"I didn't say you couldn't. Just best not to mix business with ...you know, non business." Taylor's coldness shocked even her.

"Oh," Catori stepped back. "Well, don't go far, I may need you tonight."

"It's my day off."

"Nobody said anything about the day. Tonight. And here's your pay." Catori tossed an envelope on the bed, filled with credits.

"Yeah," Taylor dragged.

"And remember why I hired you. Why I *initially* hired you," Catori said before she closed the door.

***

Taylor and Ai walked down the long, dark tunnel towards the bright lights and smoked-filled arena. The discotheque seemed bigger and more expansive as Lady Kitty stood onstage gyrated between two people. Video cameras projected her image on screens around the discotheque.

Mai walked down to meet them on the floor. She hugged Taylor and kissed her on the cheek, "Good to see you here. I was worried you were not coming back."

"It's good to be seen, you know?" Taylor laughed. "Can we go upstairs and talk for a bit? Catch up on old times."

Mai smiled and beckoned for Taylor to follow her as Ai worked his way behind the bar. He flirted with the young bartender with cybernetic arms covered with tattoos. The bartender tossed bottles in the air, making a show of mixing drinks for two college girls, obviously not from the Lowers.

Mai opened the door to a small office. Taylor walked by her and sat on a small couch next to a wall. She ran her hands through her now shoulder-length black hair and leveled her eyes on Mai.

"You look good." Mai stated as she sat.

"You look even better," Taylor leaned into the conversation.

"Liar. I'm at work all the time. I'm sure I look like a pale ghost of a person." Mai shifted on the couch.

"I don't know." Taylor licked her lips and ran her hand over Mai's cheek, "Skin like porcelain. Eyes the color of chocolate and lips...well, you know how I feel about you, Mai."

"I know you are a ruthless flirt who doesn't know when to stop." Mai laughed. "How is it being an 'I Broker'?"

"I'm just her bodyguard. Nothing major." Taylor reached down and steadied Mai's fidgeting hands. "Why are you so nervous? Confidence looks good on you."

Mai giggled a bit, a change from her normal "steely" façade. "Why don't you go join Ai for a dance on the floor. You know we will comp for drinks. And you are always welcome back here...whenever."

"Thanks." A long beep interrupted them and Taylor checked her gauntlet, "Shit."

"Duty calls? I can step out."

Taylor motioned for Mai to stay seated as she answered, "Yes, boss."

Catori barked an address. "Meet me there when you're done. I need for you to step up."

"Sure, boss." As Taylor reached over to end the call, she heard Catori speak again.

"Taylor?"

"Yeah?"

"Remember why I hired you." Catori ended the call.

Taylor glanced at Mai, "Maybe I will have that drink."

Mai walked over to the door and opened it for Taylor to go downstairs.

* * *

A sleek, black car pulled up to the curb and Taylor jumped in. She rode, alone, to the address Catori gave her. She laid back and let the liquor run through her veins and relax her. She hoped the job wouldn't be difficult, after all she was just the bodyguard.

There was a huge gate with several men wearing swords in front of it. They waved the black car through to the docks on the other side of the warehouse. As the car slowed to a stop, Taylor saw Catori speaking to a Japanese man. He also wore a sword strapped to his waist, which was unique. Taylor sat in the car for a moment and took in the scene.

Catori stood talking to the Japanese man.

"Inside." The Japanese man motioned toward a green door on the docks of the warehouse.

"Most appreciated." Catori bowed low and the man reciprocated.

Taylor stepped out of the car as the man walked away. On the dock were five other Japanese men with swords. One of them crossed his arms as he looked down at Taylor.

She wanted to ask Catori what was going on, but she blindly followed and didn't utter a sound.

They walked up a set of stairs and inside the building. Beyond the darkness surrounding them was a cone of light and a person sitting in a chair. Their head was bowed forward and their hands were tied behind the chair. The sound of their footsteps echoed. Catori led, Taylor followed and they both stopped at the edge of the light.

Taylor's eyes went to the chair and the person. She studied the woman, who was hunched over and unmoving. The woman's eyes were covered and her mouth was gagged. As Taylor moved closer, there was a pit in her stomach. The hair was curlier and more grey. The skin had lost some of its color but she knew the person, and it made her uncomfortable.

She glared at Catori and motioned, "What is this? Why is she here?"

"Work."

Taylor tried to walk out the room, but another man with a sword stepped in her path. He shook his head and pointed at the woman.

"That's *my* mother. I'm not doing anything on or to her!"

"Why not? She kicked you out! She didn't tell you about your power!" Catori clasped her hands together and touched her nose with her index fingers. "I've worked so hard to get us here. I need for you to understand. The fight was staged. Everything was done so I could get close to you."

Taylor thought back and realized Catori was calm and in control during the fight. She could have taken those guys sooner but her motions were just for show.

"No," Taylor exhaled. "No, you couldn't possibly…"

"Information is my business. Think of having someone like you with me. Think of the power and the things we could do!" Catori walked over to Taylor's mother, grabbed her hair and yanked her head backwards.

Taylor's mother groaned. She realized Catori had a point, but this was her mother. As long as there was space between them, Taylor didn't care what she did. She simply didn't care.

"I'm not going to do it." Taylor crossed her arms and stood her ground, "I'm not going to do it, Catori."

Catori made a screeching noise as she pushed Taylor's mother's head forward, "Dammit! You're not gonna do this to me."

"What she got that you want?" Taylor began mimicking Catori as they walked in a circle around Taylor's mother.

"I wanted you. She just has *information*. Doesn't matter what it is. She has it. I want it."

"Have you tried…"

"Look at her fucking face! Look at her! We've been working her for days and nothing! Now, get over here and do it!" Catori pointed downward.

Taylor stood, confused and angry. She looked at Catori. She saw men with swords step from the shadows. She didn't have the skills to beat everyone in the room. She would never make it out alive and yet, extracting information would make all the difference. She could lie. She could say there was nothing there. Her brain ran over a million scenarios.

"There's no way out. This is the endgame. Do it."

"It's all about power with you. Power and manipulation and lies!" Taylor stepped in front of her mother. "This is what you want."

"Get the information for me and great things will happen. Great things for both of us. Now, get it done." Catori's voice calmed as she pulled out a cigarette and lit it.

Taylor stood in front of her mother and slowly pulled the blindfold off. She slipped the gag out of her mouth.

Her mother started pleading, "Please. I can't see and I can't hear but I need for you to help me. Help me before the woman comes back."

Taylor glanced at the dried blood from her mother's ears. Her face was bruised. One of her eyes was swollen shut. Taylor reached into each ear and pulled out wads of cotton. She remembered the last time she saw her mother was walking down the street holding the hand of a small child. Taylor hid behind a building and watched them as a tinge of jealousy washed over her.

She looked down at her mother as she remembered. She opened her mouth to speak but choked back a guttural noise. She looked at Catori smoking. She saw the men with their swords and she shook out her arms. She stretched her neck and looked side to side.

Her right hand closed as she hit a button in her palm. She armed her cybernetic arm. Whatever happened, she wouldn't go down without a fight. With her right hand, she grabbed her mother's hair and pulled her head back so her mother could look her in the face.

"Ma. Can you see me? Can you hear me?"

"Taylor?" her voice cracked. "Baby, it's been so long."

Taylor stroked her mother's hair. "Yeah, it's been awhile, Ma."

With one good eye, her mother stared up at her. Taylor looked down on her mother for what felt like an eternity.

"There's so many things. . ." her mother began.

"Ma, don't."

"Why are you doing this? Why are you working with them? Do you know who these people are?"

"No. What do you have that they want? They want me to get the information out of you the way that I do. You never told me how to control my power. You never did anything for me..." Taylor vibrated with anger, "You had another kid and lived like I never existed."

"You ran away. We looked. What did you want us to do? Wait for you to come back?" Her mother's voice was strained. Almost a whisper.

Taylor was shocked when a tear rolled down her cheek. It fell onto her mother's face, "Sorry, Ma. It's business, not personal."

"Do what you have to do." There was the coldness Taylor knew.

Taylor sighed. Catori turned and watched. The men

moved back into the shadows as Taylor grabbed more of her mother's hair in her hand and pulled her head back...she pulled it...and pulled it until there was a snap.

She broke her neck.

Catori opened her mouth as the men leapt from the shadows. Taylor held her right arm up and unleashed a barrage of pulses towards them, disintegrating parts of their bodies in the air. Catori ran up on her and tried to grab her but Taylor stopped her with one strong punch.

The groans of the men filled the warehouse. She looked at her mother's dead body in the chair, her head dangling behind the chair. She didn't know what to do. Catori was passed out on the floor. The men were in no shape to fight. She untied her mother's body and laid it on the floor.

She dragged Catori's body to the chair and tied her up. As Catori sat, Taylor walked around the room and finished off the men. She scanned their bodies. Some of them had cybernetic parts, others did not. She was confused as to why they carried swords and yet they wore modern clothes.

"They have a sense of honor. They follow the code of the Yakuza. Loyal to the end. They also worship the way of the samurai and eschew most modern tech," Catori mumbled.

"Well, what are we gonna do?" Taylor grabbed one of the swords and walked over to Catori, "What are we gonna do?"

Catori straightened and stared into the darkness. "You take my information and become *the* new broker? The one with all the knowledge. All the power down here."

"All I wanted was to just live my life, you know? My parents kicked me out and I lived on the streets. I finally get my shit together and you just happen to drop in.

"I have to say, the temptation to drain you of all your precious information and become my own 'I Broker' is strong. I could rule the 'Lowers', run it with an iron fist. Power. All the power would be mine. And *that* would make me as despicable as you." Taylor ran her hands through her hair, "Which brings us back to, what are we gonna do, Catori?"

"You have the power now. If I were you, I'd take my information and make myself *one rich bitch*. But you aren't like me. There's no hunger in your eyes. There's nothing in your eyes, matter of fact. So, just come on and suck my soul out and try to find something you can use."

Taylor stood and looked down on Catori.

"Do it! Fucking do it!" Catori yelled.

Taylor thought. She stared at her and thought, "Back to sleep." Taylor punched Catori and knocked her out.

"What to do?" Taylor looked around the warehouse.

***

Taylor sat in the office and watched the cameras with Ai. Ai pointed out the detectives coming into the discotheque. Taylor walked out of the office and met them at the top of the stairs. She opened an office door and motioned for them to go inside.

"Do you have anything else to add?" One of the detectives lit a cigarette.

"We don't smoke in here." Taylor's tone was curt.

The detective dragged on the cigarette and kept smoking.

"I told you. I worked for her, but I was off that night. I was feeling nostalgic and took a walk." Taylor shrugged her shoulders, "Nothing to it."

The second detective looked at his partner and took over. "Thing is, we checked the cameras and we don't see any trace of you until *after* the fire. Where were you before then?"

Taylor thought back to the night at the warehouse.

Catori was tied to a chair and knocked out. Taylor

walked through the warehouse looking for accelerants, something to start a fire and clear out the evidence. She found paint thinner, linseed oil and broken wood pallets. She got to work and waited for Catori to wake.

"I'm leaving. You will die here and I'm leaving. See, I've got this little laser on my cyber arm here and I've severed some things so you can't talk. Or scream or thrash around." Taylor made a circling motion with her hand. "I also found your camera. Gone."

Catori tried to open her mouth to speak.

"What don't you get? Stay quiet. There's no trace of anything. And don't worry about the headache, you won't be alive long enough for it to matter." Taylor walked over to the doorway. She held up her arm and shot a steady laser to ignite the accelerants.

She snapped out of her thoughts when one of the detectives cleared his throat, "Sorry, Detective Anderson, I was just lost in my thoughts. I've got nothing to add."

She stood and walked around the desk. She opened the door and motioned for them to leave, "And do tell Betty that we would love to have one of her delicious old-school pies she makes. It's hard to get real food around here."

Detective Anderson leapt to his feet. The other detective clamped a hand on his shoulder, "Rob, calm down."

They walked toward the door and Taylor stretched her arm in front of them, blocking the door.

"How are the girls, Detective Rivers? Here's hoping your wife finally has that boy you've been wanting. Either way, you'll be outnumbered until she can have another one. However, with your salary, looks like you won't be having any more kids after him.

"Not unless you go back to shaking down junkies in the Lowers again. I'm sure you don't want your new boss to find out." Taylor moved her arm and the men shuffled past.

"All good here?" Ai stepped out of the camera room

as Mai walked up the stairs, and passed the detectives.

"All good. I've got a feeling they won't be back."

REGRET ME NOT

By Ava Silurian.

Through the glass wall of the conference room, Zoilix watched her intern trip and fall, sending a laden tray of piping hot something flying through the air.

Zoilix cleared her throat and refocused on the board members gathered before her. "I'm taking the company. I'll announce tomorrow. I've already sent my comments on the press release to Landl."

The room filled with clapping, and faces, the ones with human lips, broke into smiles.

Zoilix looked out at them, sat at the wavering table, its glasstic top spinning newsreels from around the world. With perfect timing, Zoilix's eyes were drawn to a news story.

[BILLIONAIRE INVENTOR, YED-SHIX, FOUNDER OF gX IMPRISONED]

Great.

Zoilix swallowed and somehow, a piece of muffin stuck in her dry throat finally made the last leg of its journey. Her throat cleared, her decision made, Zoilix was committed. She would take the helm of gX.

* * *

Zoilix's brow glittered with sweat, encased in moisture by the constant mugginess of the city. The press conference was held in a tent, a hastily assembled half-carbon fiber dome under the dark purple sky.

She stood at the front of the crowd, Landl to her right. An army of news bots hovered in front of her. She didn't know where to look. There was no one to make eye contact with anymore.

She looked down at the statement she'd prepared, from the story relayed to her by a flushed Yed-Shix just hours before.

Their video conference was allowable because Yed-Shix paid her way into the top echelon of the prison system.

"Z, you have to tell them the real story," Yed-Shix said. Behind her, a robo-cleaner maneuvered a vacuum, and fresh roses adorned the table.

Zoilix sighed. "And what's the real story, E?"

"You know Elio has been after my tech. Gregarian stole my idea for the space telecom. He stole it! I still don't know how he did it. The fucker. But I was getting ready to expose him. I had some dirt. Some real bad dirt." Yed-Shix pounded the table and the roses to her right jumped with the impact. A thought crossed Zoilix's mind. *Were those real roses? And really, did her sister—the attempted murderer— really get real-rose-star-treatment?*

"Of course. He's a monster." Zoilix's script was flawless. It was a constant necessity when dealing with the evil demons, real and imagined, that plagued her sister's life.

"Tell them the real story! Free me! Get me out of this

fucking place!"

It was not like Yed-Shix to beg. Zoilix shifted in her chair and couldn't look her in the eye. "I will, I promise you," Zoilix said into her lap. She fiddled with the blue gold comm-path on the palm of her right hand. She had a sudden urge to press it, to end the call with her sister. *What about me?* Zoilix thought.

And the question came back to her, later, at the press conference. *What about me?* She had not had any oxygen while near her larger-than-life sister. Not since they were young. The mechanic-turned-genius-slash-inventor sister. The woman with her bright eyes and winning smile, somehow always covered in oil, or charred lubricant, tinkering with something, be it a motor or your purse, or your heart.

What about me?

"Esteemed press," Zoilix said, sweeping her arm up and out. Assorted chirps and bleeting notes from the robo-press. "Yed-Shix, my genius twin sister, founder of gX Technologies, has been wrongly accused and imprisoned. She has been targeted by the predatory Gregarian, who stole her line of GiGi-HandFloats, claiming it to be his own invention. He has profited from her work, stealing her ideas for years, and now, framed her in his own-" and here, Zoilix added air quotes "assassination attempt."

Zoilix swallowed, her mouth dry. She wiped her gleaming brow, rubbing her hand on her trousers. "Gregarian, and his evil corporation, profit from child labor, mind you!" Zoilix's voice cracked. "He and his corporation are profiting on the backs of innocents, all the while he steals and he cheats and he gets away with it. Do not make the mistake of empathizing with this monster."

She stepped down from the podium.

"Good job," Landl said, patting her on the back.

"Ughhhh," Zoilix's shoulders caved as she walked off the stage with Landl. They crossed an area congested with people, waiting in line. It was a lighting press round: controversies abounded, and each person in line waited for their turn to address the press.

"Let's get a drink, okay?" Landl's warm voice released a small bit of tension from Zoilix's shoulders.

Too bad he's married, she thought, for the infinitieth time. Her crush on Landl had grown and waned over the years, but a constant coal of love always burned deep in her belly.

They walked out of the dome, across the street to the pub. Upon entering, they were accosted by loud tech binary, what some called "music". Apparently the robo-rave had been raging since two weeks ago, when the courts declared robo-bodiez a form of consciousness, and thus party to the same human rights as their biological relatives. Zoilix grimaced. She and Landl turned around, to find another bar, where they could actually hear each other.

They stepped out into the street, the automatic swarm of umbrella dog-bots, hungry for tips, accosted them. It never stopped raining. Plants and moss everywhere, grimy molds grew on every possible surface, somehow immune to the heavy metals in the rain. They loved it. The molds evolved so much some species had produced tiny almost-legs. Zoilix kept a particularly close eye on a colony latched to her bedroom window that she was sure wasn't far off from reaching consciousness and demanding equal rights and housing.

The two of them bundled into a bar, much quieter than the first, with large moth-eaten sofas. The place, Vintig, prided itself on its past-loving aesthetic. They even had one of the first models of a computer, encased in a thick glasstic prism floating in the center of the circular bar.

Landl and Zoilix flopped down on a mustard-colored chaise lounge. Zoilix laughed as she watched dust rise from it. Prided themselves on authenticity, *indeed*.

"You did good. Really good. I felt like Yed-Shix was actually some sort of martyr. The tears! The shouting! Awesome."

"But, she is?"

Landl's face broke into a smile. "Oh Zoi, you poor used-up soul."

"She's been framed! Gregarian is fucking evil!"

Landl didn't answer, he just watched Zoilix's face.

Zoilix loved when Landl focused on her eyes. But now, he studied her like a cold and removed scientist, poking at her. She was the drugged-up rat in a maze, wondering which way led to final comfort. "I know you're not the biggest fan of my sister."

Landl's lips curled inwards, like he held in a giggle. He reached down, took a pillow from the chaise lounge, and hugged it to his chest. He watched Zoilix.

A cloud of tired descended on Zoilix. In these few weeks since her sister had been imprisoned, she felt this new heavy burden of the company.

A chirp from her hand comm: she pressed a button on it, and a text appeared across her eyesight.

<Urgent message for Zoilix Sishanur>

Zoilix blinked and the message opened on the screen across her retinas.

<Hello darling. It's lovely to meet you. You can call me K. Now that our lovely Miss Yed is in the brig, you will be the one to send me my weekly credit infusion. I'm so looking forward to this new working relationship! I'm sure we're going to have so very much fun. (devil emoji)>

Zoilix closed the message tab and looked at Landl, processing the text.

"Did you just get a message from someone named "K"?" He said.

She nodded.

"I knew it!" Landl stood up, his face turned red under the half plate of tech that covered his left eye, the left eye he lost in the war. "She's taking their money. God, she really is a piece of shit!"

"Hey!" Zoilix stood up. "That's my sister you're talking about. Your boss, the one who has gainfully employed you for years, OK? Who scraped you out of that shithole masquerading as a factory?"

"Zoi. I knew she was bad news. But if she is taking money from the Association…"

"Wait, hold on. She's taking money from the Association? The Association?" Zoilix sat back down. Little pinpricks of rainbow light swarmed in her vision, her heart beating fast. "The Association."

"I was going to retire this year. I was going to leave all of this, with Tabitha. Never to see Yed-Shix's viper face, never again. We were finally going to be free. Find a place out in the sticks, with a farm and our own *vegetables*. Maybe a few goats."

"What the hell is a 'goat'?" The word felt harsh in Zoilix's mouth.

Landl didn't answer. His half-metal face was in his hands. He sighed.

"We're totally fried, aren't we?" Zoilix ran her hand across the back of her neck, squeezing it in a vain attempt to release some tension.

"We *are* fried. If Yed-Shix has been paying off the Association, we are ready to be baked to a crisp. May as well sign our death certificate now, Zoi."

"No goating for you."

"It's- it's not a verb. But yes," he wagged his head, adding a hollow guffaw. "No goating for me."

* * *

Later, they were back at the office. They looked through the mountain of files, searching through to find the evidence. It took them a few hours, but finally, they uncovered it: the gold mine, all of Yed-Shix's communications with "K", all of the credits she funneled to them.

Zoilix munched on a protein bar, reconstituted from the new moss strains that had evolved in the city, probably the same kind that populated her window. She wondered in a flash, how long it would take before this could still be considered vegetarian. Her stomach rebelled and she thought for a minute that she might be sick. But she closed her eyes, swallowed, willed it to stay down. After a moment, the feeling passed. She leaned over the desk, hovering behind Landl as he dug through the files.

They truly were fried.

With all of the Association's clout, with all of their drug money, with all the behind-the-scenes puppetry controlling the government; there was nowhere for Zoilix and Landl to go. Not now that they knew what they knew. If they tried to run, or go to the press, "K" would have them chopped to bits, incinerated in a reactor before the day reached its end.

The buzzer rang; someone was at the door. It was after business hours.

What the hell?

Zoilix and Landl looked at each other, panicked. Landl reached down to the table, pressing the display button on his console. On the screen, a video came to light. At the front door to the office, stood a horde, at least 15 men.

Zoilix screamed. "Check the back cameras."

Landl switched views to the back exit, down the narrow hallway, through the central factory floor. Guys there too. He flicked between each camera, each one packed with shadowy figures.

"We're trapped. We can't, we can't." Zoilix backed over to the wall, pressed her back against it and slid to the floor.

Landl came over to her. "I armed the system. That will keep them out for about 30 minutes." He reached out, touched her arm. "Zoilix, seeing as it is the end of the world for us… I wanted to ask you," he paused, "Do you know how beautiful you are?"

Zoilix's head snapped up to meet his gaze. She could see his robotic eye was filled with molten redness, flowing like a glittering lava field. The other half of his face, his strong jaw, those eyes, directed on her. Her whole body felt aligned, and all she was, was that moment, that one moment when Landl was looking into her. She reached up and put a hand on his face.

He leaned down and kissed her. The metal of half of his lips sent an exciting, arctic chill down her spine. This moment kissing Landl was everything she dreamt it to be. She pulled his arms around her and grabbed him, tried to pull all of him closer to her. She couldn't get enough.

And as they melted into each other, the building rocked with an explosion.

* * *

Through the glass wall of the conference room, Zoilix watched her intern trip and fall, sending a laden tray of piping hot something flying through the air.

Zoilix cleared her throat and refocused on the board members gathered before her. "I'm leaving the company. Landl can take over for us both. The sisters are out, I'm going to spend my time trying to get Yed-Shix out of prison. Good luck. I know you'll do a great job, Landl."

Zoilix looked out at them, sat at the wavering table, its glasstic top spinning newsreels from around the world. With perfect timing, Zoilix's eyes were drawn to a news story.

[BILLIONAIRE INVENTOR, YED-SHIX, FOUNDER OF gX IMPRISONED]

Great.

Landl's face was bright and excited. The rest of the board said little, save for one member. A purple robo-bodie wrapped around her upper torso, she clapped.

Zoilix nodded at Landl. Her decision made, she was committed.

* * *

After, Zoilix and Landl stood outside the conference room.

"You can do this," Zoilix said. "You're going to lead this company much better than I ever could, I'm sure of it. You were closer to the tech side of my sister. You *got* her." At this, tears sprung into Zoilix's eyes. She blushed, rubbing her eyes, and looked down.

"I'm truly honored. I- This is just so much to think about. I've never run an entire company. And I only worked with your sister on developing the tech. I don't have any vision/insight with regards to the business side, I really don't."

Zoilix waved her hand. "It's fine. You're surrounded by the best, Friy knows absolutely everything there is to know about finances. Once he's back from the moon trip, he'll be able to download it all to you in no time."

She looked into Landl's face, the bright red of his beard like a fire scar. She longed to reach out and touch it. *Landl. Landl. Landl.* His voice was a constant talisman that flashed through her mind.

"OK, wow." Landl puffed out his cheeks. He rubbed his arms and looked down the hallway, towards the conference room, out of which the board members now filtered. The meeting was over, the news announced.

"I promise you, it's going to be fine." Zoilix said.

* * *

At home, Zoilix packed a bag with a few of her key possessions. She would sleep outside her lawyer's office if she had to. Penny Friglan was the company lawyer, and she only worked strict business hours. But Zoilix needed her, right away. She could get Yed-Shix out of the bind she was in.

Zoilix packed her pod. The collapsable, and then re-inflatable, metallic exoskeleton—given out as a relief to those living in the toxic streets of the Arc. The pods protected a human body from the moss that would grow, unhindered, if one were to stay outside for longer than an hour. Moss-eaten corpses were found each year, more than bodies torn apart with bullets, or swords. Even the rats wouldn't touch a corpse the moss had conquered. *Even the rats.*

Her items packed, her heart ready, Zoilix left her 198th floor apartment. Up at this level, the altitude equalizers were top notch. The co-founder of a tech company had the best. Zoilix looked out onto her living space, before she turned off the lights. Sleek, minimal, beautiful.

She took the hover-vator down to the lobby, passed the constantly playing gambling rings (the lobby was also a casino). Robo-bodiez adorned most of the crowd, who were rich enough to afford the expensive life-extending body parts.

Zoilix deployed her body suit before stepping out into the rain. Even through the suit, she could feel the heat of it, its constant drumming. She hailed a taxi.

From the window of the taxi, as they flew across the city, Zoilix watched the towering spires of buildings whiz past, clustered like druids. The taxi's current altitude was not congested: it was off-peak, so they made good time.

They came to the outskirts, and the taxi stopped at a short, skinny building, only 500 stories tall: the center of legal progress for the city. Across the street was the jail.

Zoilix turned to look at the looming complex, where her sister was housed. She imagined her, lounging in her ritz tower.

Zoilix walked up the ele-steps to the front of the building. Next to the entrance doors, there was a robo guard, powered down. Zoilix wondered why: this would be a useless piece of tech, a guard without any power.

Zoilix unfurled the pod and it exploded into its usual shape in front of her. Though it started as a stress ball sized cube, pulsing and giving off light; deployed, it stood ten feet tall.

When it deployed, Zoilix realized her mistake. The

robo-guard snapped to life and issued an alarm. It motored over to Zoilix, clearly not there to listen or to empathize. After a few minutes, the front doors of the legal building burst open and out came Penny. She frowned at Zoilix.

"You know my robot almost vaporized your sorry ass, right?" she said, crossing her arms and laughing.

"Hi Penny. I didn't think you'd be here."

"This is where I live," Penny said.

"But, Yed-Shix? Her hearing?"

"Yeah, I sent Sam. He needs the experience." Penny leaned over and pressed a button on the side of the droid. A retina scanner telescope extended. Penny leaned down, putting her eyeball close to be scanned.

Satisfied, the robot calmed, sped back to its post, and powered down.

Zoilix sighed, relieved that her ears were no longer filled with the wail of the alarm.

"OK, Z, come on in then. Let's talk options."

Zoilix followed Penny into the building. At 500 floors, it was one of the several grand mansions of the city. Penny, one of the top lawyers (if not *the* top lawyer), could afford it, with her clout. Penny and her partner lived on the top 10 floors, their law offices the 20 floors below that. Zoilix never asked what the remaining 470 floors were used for. Probably better left unasked.

They shot up to the 490th floor. The elevator opened onto the grand entrance, an entire floor devoted to a series of fountains. A spa filled the left wing of this floor, a scent of menthol hanging in the air.

Penny sailed through the main entrance way and up the escalator. The escalator sliced up through all 10 floors, to the extensive garden on the roof. The dome above the garden simulated the sun, protecting the tropical paradise from the toxic rain.

Penny was silent. She looked at Zoilix once, frowned, and turned away.

Up on the garden level, Zoilix squinted in the onslaught of the intense bright light. The synthetic sun singed her skin.

Getting off the escalator, they followed a rocky path to an opulent lounge area, with a fully-stocked bar, lounge chairs, a tree house and all throughout robotic servants cleaning and tidying.

Penny sat down at a table and motioned for Zoilix to sit next to her. One of the robots came to take their order.

"Blood and ginger," Penny said.

Drinking blood was the newest fad of the elite, engineered from a lab-created monstrosity. It was composed of goose and pig, a creature you would not want to see.

"Water," Zoilix said, when the servant turned to her. It sped away, and a moment later, was back with the tray of drinks.

Penny put the ruby drink to her lips. "Oh Zoilix. The other half of the superstar sisters. About to camp out in front of my home."

Zoilix took a sip of her water. And just then, a ping rang out in her comms system.

<Receiving Video Transmission>

"You can put it up on the screen here," Penny said. She reached down one of the table legs, and a video screen rose from the table top.

Zoilix blinked, transferring the message onto the screen.

Just like Penny's drink, the video was bloody. A gray room, and in the middle, Landl was tied up in glowing chains. He had been stripped naked. Pulled into a gruesome spread eagle, hanging in the middle of the cell. A robot was in the process of whipping him with a silvery cord.

A cheery narrator started in: "Hello Zoilix! It's just so lovely to make your acquaintance!" The narration cut out, in favor of Landl's screams.

Zoilix turned white. She looked at Penny. Penny looked back at her and continued sipping her drink.

"Just wow, lovely to meet you. Your sister has told me such wonderful things.

Well, enough about you. I'm K." K paused again, in time for the robot to take a whirring saw to Landl's side, scraping out a chunk of flesh. Another robot followed with a red hot cauterizing machine, stopping the blood, but surely not the pain.

Zoilix gasped, and with a flailing hand, knocked her water to the ground. The water spilled out over the rocks below.

"Stop, stop," Zoilix breathed, watching the man she loved being carved out and mangled. "Stop!" she shouted.

"Oh Zoilix, now I have your attention! This is how it's going to go. You're going to take over the company, and we're going to work together from now on. It's going to be delightful! I truly cannot wait!"

Landl squealed, as the robot stuck a rod through his finger.

Zoilix felt her hand tingle. "OK, OK, STOP HURTING HIM! I'll do what you say, I'll do exactly what you say."

Penny chimed in, across the table, "Good choice Z, good choice."

* * *

Zoilix stepped out of the Regret-Me-Not machine. Her head spun and she fell onto the laminated floor of the factory. She retched, bringing nothing up. Trying to recover her breath, she stood up and considered.

Her sister had just been imprisoned. One day ago.

And Zoilix saw that she had no other option but to flee. Her sister had done enough. She had built this company into the evil, illegal corner it was in. Yed-Shix was responsible, not Zoilix.

For just one moment, she considered staying, trying to help her sister escape yet another bind. Their old, tired dynamic.

But no, enough was enough.

Zoilix took a deep breath, and chose *Zoilix*.

She fired off a quick anonymous message to Landl. Telling him to turn the company in to the cops and flee. He would have time to save himself and Tabitha. She hoped.

Zoilix would risk escaping down through the sewer system. It wasn't monitored as closely as the vehicles in and out of the city.

Suddenly, a square of light was thrown into the room as a door at the other side of the factory floor opened. Zoilix heard voices.

No time, had to run.

She raced to the edge of the room, ducking down into the mechanical room. She closed the door behind her, trying to stay as quiet as possible. She whirled around, crossed the room to the sewer grating. She pulled it up, and climbed down the rungs of the ladder that led into the dark hole. It didn't smell too bad.

Yet.

She reached up, and pulled the sewer grate down. She slid down the ladder, stopping herself a few times, to make sure she didn't crash too hard into the ground below. Down she flew as the tiny circle of light above her disappeared.

Finally, she hit the floor. Thankfully, the floor appeared to be dry. The smell had worsened, though.

She was in a cavern, barely as tall as she was. Muted lighting shone on the walls. She looked around, holding up part of her shirt to block the smell. There was a passageway to the right, and another to the left.

Yet again, a decision.

Zoilix closed her eyes, and took a deep breath. She thought of Landl, his name echoing through her mind. The man she loved, the only man she'd ever loved. She opened her eyes, decided. She would take the passageway to the right.

I wonder if I'll get to do some goating, she thought, and walked into the darkness.

FELK THE NETWORK

By Amber Benbow.

Layleanna flung her right arm—her real arm—across the bed in a panic. It connected with the firm mattress, and she curled her fingers into the sheets. Sweat dampened the base of her neck, though the room itself was cool. She listened to the galloping of her heart as it drowned out the last images of her dream. The fingers of her left hand stretched and curled in a rhythm outside her will. Slowly, she was able to regain control. She felt a tingling sensation as though her left arm had fallen asleep for a few moments. Of course, it had no blood since it was her mech arm. She had chosen the dark gray sythen-skin to stand out as a stylish accessory.

Sirens drifted distantly through her room. It was dark still, and the gray glow of city lights bounced off the open closet and bare walls. Her heartbeat was settling and the grip of her dream loosened. Layleanna rolled her eyes upward into the blackness of the internet to check the time and her messages.

Three a.m.? Ain't gonna happen.

With a sigh, she pushed herself from the bed, grabbing her robe from the corner of the bedroom door. Layleanna knew when she dreamed about losing control of her cybernetic arm it would result in a sleepless night. The hacking had left her unable to trust anything other than her own flesh and blood.

Her foot hit an unopened cardboard box in the kitchen. She swore and searched out a light switch. Through squinted eyes, she surveyed the current layout and then snapped the light off. Two days ago she had moved into her new corporate digs with Walker Global. It was the nicest place she had ever lived. The smell of fresh pine and drywall were present beneath the odor of her personal belongings. The carpet and linoleum were new, and it had all the new features including the nosy home assistant and interactive walls.

Her interviewer and soon-to-be boss, Mr. Karumi, had offered her an apartment that was partially furnished when he found out she was living in the Honami district. "These accommodations will be better than you have previously known," he had stated with a smirk.

She had bowed her head in acknowledgement. She had no doubt that was true given the reputation of the Honomi district in Arc city. "Thank you, Mr. Karumi. I am honored to accept a position at Walker Global and to live in such fine accommodations."

Layleanna snaked her way through the unpacked maze, the image of it held perfectly in her mind. She took a mug down from the cabinet and put it in the dispenser machine, groping around for a button. The entire machine was smooth and sleek. There wasn't a suggestion of a button or keypad.

"How'd you…damn thing…"

Before she could reach for a light, a voice asked, "What would you like, Ms. Graves?"

"Water," she croaked, sweeping her blonde hair out of her face. Layleanna had not accounted for the fact some essential functions of her apartment would be controlled by the assistant.

Water poured into her mug. Layleanna downed it in a few gulps and put it back in the dispenser. "Coffee."

Steaming mug in hand, she whiled away the hours unpacking. The repetitive, simple work soothed her nerves. In a few hours, she would start at Walker Global, the cybernetic technology pioneer with a reputation for using employees until they burned out... which had also offered her an astonishingly generous salary and benefits package. Not that this was the reason for her seeking employment there. She had been instructed by Omni Corp's Board of Directors to obtain a software management project at Walker Global in order to loosen the grasp Walker held over the increasing transhumanist movement. She merely had to release a bot into the system to stop their takeover.

Easy peasy, lemon squeezy. Or so the Board of Directors implied. Layleanna wasn't naive; she realized how risky and nearly impossible such a task was. Playing corporate espionage could cost her life.

After years of working for Omni, the uncertainty of starting at another company gnawed at Layleanna.

The gray of the morning receded from the apartment as the boxes dwindled. Still, Layleanna found she had more time than things to do. Boredom outweighed hesitation and caution. She curled up on an overstuffed chair with her tablet. With a few taps, she entered into her AI playground, where Felk was eager to greet her. She smiled at his fuzzy form and large, cartoon eyes. Each time she logged on, he had changed slightly as he developed a sense of self. He was the most advanced AI she had designed and Layleanna was becoming deeply attached to him.

Layleanna sipped her coffee while she lost herself in his training.

***

Approaching the Walker Global headquarters, Layleanna was taken aback at how stunning the building was. It caught red shards of the morning sun and radiated it back in rainbows. The building stood out like a diamond in the morning haze.

Inside, her boots clicked on the polished tile floors of the lobby. A new wave of anxiety welled up in her. This time, it left a tight knot at the back of her throat. *Pull yourself together! This is nothing but a fresh start at a new company,* she reassured herself.

She knew the beginning would be the hardest. It would take time to learn her role and how to interact with the development team. She took a deep breath and turned into the office she had interviewed in.

"Good morning, Mr. Kurami."

A petite man sat at a glass desk. Over his eye was a piece of plexiglass. From Layleanna's angle, she caught a glimpse of the text rolling rapidly across it. His gaze was distant, but snapped to her when she entered.

"Ah, you are here so early. Please have a seat and we will be with you momentarily."

Layleanna sat in his office lounge sipping another cup of coffee. Her fifth cup of the day was a nerve-soothing temperature, though she knew it was an illusion. Each cup had put her increasingly on edge. Waiting for Mr. Karumi, Layleanna rolled back her eyes and began checking messages and apps. Her eyelids twitched over her prominent cheekbones.

Though she was immersed in her online life, she was partly aware of time passing. *I wonder how long before he's ready? Surely an early arrival wouldn't throw a company like this off?*

"Ms. Graves."

Layleanna broke off her connection and looked at Mr. Karumi standing in the doorway of his office.

"Yes?"

"Here is your employee identification card which you will need to grant you access to your work area, the cafeteria and restaurant downstairs, as well as hail a coach. Keep it with you at all times. Now, uh, shall we start with the tour?"

"That sounds fabulous."

She followed Mr. Karumi from his executive suite. It looked out over the entirety of Walker's headquarters. The hallways wrapped around the edge of the building, leaving the middle open with an impressive view to the lobby 40 floors below. That was where the pool with a fountain and plants rested. Layleanna could hear the calming ripple of water over stones and smell the freshness of plants. It was strikingly pleasant compared to the humidity outside.

Along their tour, she saw many employees hurrying through the halls, everyone with deep grimaces across their faces. When they arrived at a set of large double glass doors, Mr. Kurami opened them for her with a bow.

"This will be your new role, Ms. Graves," he said. "You will be overseeing the software development of all of our cybernetics. Of course, we want you to focus on the high-end clients who will be ordering custom pieces, but we have provided you with a team who will be responsible for the updating of the older models as well."

Layleanna swept her eyes through the room. She estimated 15 employees were scattered throughout 35 terminals. The terminals were large cushioned chairs that reclined almost flat. This provided a comfortable receptacle for the employee's body while their mind wrote or tested code. Layleanna observed a few finger and eye twitches as they stared unseeingly into the ceiling. Their tiny movements were the only indication they were writing code at all.

"Where are the rest of them?" She asked about the half-empty terminals.

Mr. Karumi inclined his head. "We do not ask that our employees keep a strict schedule of work hours, instead we ask them to meet quotas. Some employees are at home having met their goals for the week." He paused, considering his words. "Others will no longer be with us here at Walker."

Layleanna's brows rose. His words felt sinister, as though more than a job were at stake.

"I hope you will educate me as to what is acceptable for myself and my employees." She sensed the quotas were unreasonable, but dismissed it. Layleanna knew she needed to focus on the mission and not righting every wrong at Walker.

He showed her to her "office". It was a standing terminal near the window where she could monitor the hours logged on each terminal. She noted one employee had logged 17 hours straight. Layleanna tisked and reached for the mandatory logout button she controlled as a manager. At Omni, a human would never to be allowed to work such grueling hours without surfacing to reality, to relieve their biological needs at the very least. Surely this man needed to pee, or eat, or anything that involved taking care of his body.

Mr. Karumi rose his hand to stop her. "He may not be able to find his place again if you log him out now. Better to indicate that he should find an acceptable stopping place and then return." He swiped the screen over and showed her an alternate button.

Layleanna compiled, tapping this button once. She tallied the corrections she would be making to their work environment while she was here. The line between biological entities and machines had become too blurred. This was a place that needed to be reminded of its humanity.

* * *

Layleanna began packing up her gear, fitting most of it into her shoulder bag. The gray of her sythen-skin blended seamlessly into the gray of her shoulder bag when she hooked her left thumb into the strap.

Two weeks in at Walker and she was already dreading coming back. Every day she was asked to wring more out of her team than they had to give. Each goal, when accomplished, revealed itself to be false and a new one took its place. Mr. Karumi was never satisfied nor proud of their accomplishments.

"How you feel is irrelevant," he had said to her when she protested. "All that matters is how well our products perform."

Unbridled rage rose up in her. She felt people should have pride in their work, should feel some contentment, and yet she knew instinctively that such humanitarian attitudes would be stamped out at Walker. Still, she found herself increasingly unable to enforce Walker's policies. When an employee asked for time off, she obliged without hesitation knowing that she would be reprimanded.

It was becoming increasingly apparent that her time at Walker would be short. At Omni, she had never felt inadequate. She put the most recent incident out of her mind. The close supervision she felt her employees needed were not on quotas, but on reconnecting with each other. Her team needed to rediscover themselves as bio entities, not machines. Though many on her team had cybernetics and other enhancements, none identified as a full transhuman—those with full body enhancements who were only one consciousness upgrade away from being a cyborg.

Thumb still tucked into her shoulder bag, Layleanna surveyed the smattering of people logged into their terminals. Two she had seen logged in when she arrived; they hadn't spoken outside of their chat boxes, since they had yet to surface to reality.

Layleanna sighed, closing the double glass doors behind her. The locks automatically snicked shut. Though Walker Global had excellent security—the best that money could buy—it would take one cyber psychotic bursting through an unlocked door to knock out her entire team.

When they were logged in they were at their most vulnerable. Their lives could be cut short before they even had a chance to react.

She strode confidently down the hall, letting the muffled sound of her heels tick rhythmically behind her. Layleanna was exhausted, but suppressed a yawn while she waited for the elevator. Out in the halls, anyone could see her and report her for being inefficient. She knew to keep her guard up.

She stepped out into the evening. A wall of humidity crashed into her, tightening her chest and clinging to her skin. Layleanna did notice the brilliant orange and reds of the setting sun through the haze of Arc. Though, between the humidity and the haze, the evening was oppressive.

The circle in front of Walker Global had a landing pad where driverless vehicles swooped in to pick up riders. Layleanna stood in a marked spot on that circle to hail a coach. She swiped her Walker ID on the coach's door handle. As part of her benefits package, she was allowed unlimited private rides on any luxury coach, ad-free. The coach's door beeped in acknowledgement and slid open.

Layleanna jumped in, her bag proceeding her. "Mmm, well hello honey," she sighed in contentment. The coach's interior arched elegantly, revealing a comfortable and cushioned lounge where all passengers could face each other. Layleanna sunk into the leather seats, requesting the vehicle turn on the cooling feature. Within moments, a tingle of cool seeped through her clothing erasing the memory of summer's stickiness. Though she despised Walker, she couldn't deny that she enjoyed the lap of luxury at Walker they provided her.

"Would you like music, Ms. Graves?" the coach asked. All of her personal information was stored on her ID card. Upon swiping, the vehicle knew her name, address, and ambiance settings. She had asked that music not be played automatically, but instead be requested.

"No." Today the thought of music felt like sandpaper

across an open wound.

"Would you like hot coffee? Tea? Water?"

"Silence." Layleanna stared out the window as the vehicle progressed forward. Each day her coach took a different route to Walker's corporate tower. All coaches communicated directly with the grid and knew when to take a more efficient route based on traffic patterns. Because of this, she was rapidly learning the layout of this end of Arc. At Omni, she had never risen high enough to be included at any level in the corporate tower. Here, even though she was a mid-ranking 52 out of 126, she had never lived in a more impressive place. She could see the luxury tower looming a few miles away. It filled up part of the front window as well as the ample sunroof.

An unexplainable feeling of dread and sadness struck her as she approached. Towers like these were the reason why the average person suffered. The fact that their extravagance were borrowed against the livelihood of the larger population turned whole knots in her stomach. Here Layleanna benefited from corporate power, having risen steadily up the ladders for the past 25 years. Each stride she made furthered her bottom line and as a result, left someone else to suffer.

The cityscape passed by, grimy and distant through the haze. Those who couldn't afford personal coaches like her own, even at the most basic, ad-incessant membership levels, were left to walk. As innocuous as that sounded, it exposed the pedestrian to the elements. Less than an hour outside unprotected could result in serious sunburns, welts and damaged clothing from acid rain or asthma attacks from prolonged exposure to smog. Those who could, purchased helmets to protect themselves. Everyone else limited exposure or suffered the consequences. Aside from being dangerous, walking was extremely time-consuming. Those at the higher level could not afford the time it would take to traverse half the city without a coach.

From her vantage point, Layleanna saw a man jogging past, closely following the lines of buildings along his right. He wore no helmet. His face and bald head were crimson from exposure and exertion, she realized. He was a burly figure who held himself with anger and purpose. Despite this, something about his movements caused her to panic. At first she couldn't place why. Then it clicked: he was traveling at nearly the same speed on foot as her coach.

Inhuman.

A more unsettling feeling washed over her and instinct drove her forward.

"Emergency stop."

Readying herself she reached for her shoulder bag, pinning it tight to her body.

The coach responded immediately, flashing red filled the cabin, then a boop-boop. The door slid open.

The man, having seen her, was running away. Layleanna pulled her gun from her bag and trained it on him. She felt as if she were outside of her body, not quite in control of herself.

"Stop! A cyber psychotic!"

Those on the street were anxiously watching. The man seemed to hear and stopped. Layleanna swallowed and gripped her gun tighter. He turned to face her.

She was beyond fear. There was only the moment: now. She knew that she must take him down before he rampaged, destroying property and taking lives. Instead, she focused on his yellowed eyes and the too many beads of sweat on his forehead which ran in streams down his mech face. His eyes darted rapidly while he returned her stare.

The heavy drumming of her heart drowned out all else.

His eyes glinted and his smile was too large for his face. She realized his face could be one of the last things she would see.

Part of her hearing registered that someone had called

District Security. *Reinforcements are on the way.* Though this did not stop her. She knew in her heart she could never allow another maniac like her son to take an innocent's life. She fought the image of her son holding a gun to the head of a convenience store clerk. His body was stiff and his gestures jerky. The footage was too grainy, but she knew his skin was yellowed and damp, too. He was consumed by Zohai, a raving lunatic who needed nothing but his next fix. Layleanna had closed her eyes and longed to brush back a lock of his dirty blond hair. To her fingers it would always be baby soft.

Zohai destroyed lives. And Layleanna wouldn't stand for it anymore. Aiming for the sole patch of damp, yellowed skin around his human eye, she pulled the trigger.

Layleanna sat on a bench as the adrenaline receded. Her thoughts were starting to surface in the chaos of the room. Around her, she saw indistinct shapes.

"Where am I?" She asked. She saw the shapes sway in response but couldn't make out words. Her own voice sounded tinny in her head.

"You're in a ramen shop, ma'am." It was a woman's voice; soft, enjoyable, and with a rich timbre.

Layleanna turned, focusing on the woman. Her hair cascaded down in twists, framing her face, with a smattering of color peeking through the dark locks. Her face was cherub round and as inviting as the night.

"Can you stand?" Hands reached out, pulling Layleanna up.

She stood with woozy feet.

"You saved him, you know."

"Lucian?" Layleanna was incredulous. Her son had been dead nearly 15 years now.

The woman furrowed her brows and pursed her lips. "Sure, whoever that boy was running from the psycho. I think he may've had some, uh, desirable goods."

"Where is Security? Won't they need to interview me?"

"Oh no. Walker's Security heads this district and is already handlin' the mess."

Layleanna shifted uncomfortably. She had acted on rash fear and instinct. Consciously, she had no idea what the man was up to, but subconsciously experience had taught her destruction rode the wake of such a man.

Picking up on her discomfort, the woman said, "Don't worry about it, you did us all a favor. Here, would you like a cup of noodles?"

Her smile was as warm and welcoming as the steam rising from the cup in her hand.

Water spilled down the synth-skin of Layleanna's arm. She could hear the gears whirring and grinding, but still she could not stop clutching the glass. The sharp smell of charged ions filled the air. Each second she was unable to let go of the broken glass her heart raced faster.

A scream escaped from her lips.

The assistant's voice asked, "What would you like me to do?"

Layleanna continued screaming, unable to respond.

"What would you like me to do?"

Finally the glitch ended and she was able to gain control of her left arm again. She loosened the fingers, dropping the glass to the floor.

"Damn, damn. Damn."

"What would you like me to do?"

"Shut up!" she snapped, sweat beading at the nape of her neck. Since she started at Walker her patience had become threadbare. "There is nothing you can do."

The glitching was becoming unbearable. She knew that she would need to correct the malfunction before she launched Felk in a few days. She couldn't afford a single misstep.

Pulling out her tablet, she logged onto the dark web. She put out a request for user ukkobiu1998. Layleanna had created her left arm using scavenged parts and custom code. Since her hack, she was too paranoid to trust a company with her livelihood. But for install? She would need a technician.

A chatbox with a strange icon popped on her screen. It held instructions on how to arrive to a designated location. The coordinates seemed familiar, though she suspected she would need to travel on foot. She left her apartment with her helmet in tow.

Following user ukkobiu1998's instructions, Layleanna hailed a coach with a prepaid card. She had set this card up using a series of false accounts and dead ends for her escape from Walker. It wasn't truly anonymous, but it wouldn't flag the attention of institutions either. She was trying to put as many barriers between her and Walker as she could.

When she entered the address into the coach's console, the windows tinted charcoal. Light that had filled the cabin faded away.

Ah, I see. Keep me blind and invisible. She rubbed her left arm where it connected with her flesh. It had stopped hurting years ago, but the habit persisted. She missed what it felt like to be entirely human.

Bored in the darkness, Layleanna laid back rolling her eyes to the internet. Her vision was met with an exclamation mark enclosed in a red triangle. *Blocked.* Her heart rate quickened and a shock of white-hot energy shot through her spine. Here she was, trapped and alone at the mercy of user ukkobiu1998. It was as though he were holding a branding iron to her breast, daring her to breathe too deeply. She did anyway, to combat the unbidden feeling of dread. It was made worse by her nakedness. Without the internet, she was nothing.

Layleanna sat suspended in this time capsule, unsure of everything. Her fear compounded every moment. Then she felt the slowing of the coach, its gentle stop, and she heard the internal locks snick open. Layleanna exited the vehicle onto jagged concrete. The thin outline of cobble stones could be seen beneath the pooling water in potholes. The cobblestones were a testament to Arc's age, though she had yet to see the evidence itself. She clenched her right hand, feeling her nails bite into her palm.

Her signal came back in a flood. Messages pinged in, though one stayed pinned above the rest; an image of a red building, peeling in places, and set in a stucco façade. A line of text below it read, *Proceed 500 ft, turn right. Enter. Await further instruction.*

Layleanna looked both ways down the street. Behind her was an empty street, torn up and partially flooded. Buildings crowded in at the sides. In front of her was a bridge hundreds of feet in the air that physically cut the district in half. High speed trains raced across it at steady intervals.

Layleanna grimaced, as this was the first time she had seen the bridge from this perspective. It felt as though all of Arc was passing the Sal district by. She attached her helmet to the top of her coat collar. A fine mist of rain was setting in, leaving smeared droplets across her vision. Outside of her coat and helmet, she was poorly dressed for this part of the city. She was used to smooth concrete and found the sound of her heels on pavement pleasingly powerful. But here those same pumps were a hazard. She placed a delicate hand on a wall and began to undo her straps. She figured sunburned and bruised, was better than a twisted ankle.

"I wouldn't do that if I were you."

Layleanna looked up startled to see a large form standing in front of her. Her first thought was of a man—big shoulders, heavy leather jacket, and gray hair cropped short. Then she noticed dark jeans clinging tightly to slight legs and underdeveloped knees. The contrast between the bulky torso and skinny legs was comical.

"At least if you want to keep your feet," the voice said.

"Are you the tech?"

"User ukkobiu1998? No, but I figured I should show

you or y'all be needing new feet." The figure gestured flippantly to her, turned, and then walked several paces down the cragged street.

Layleanna let go of the shoe strap, her face puckered in confusion. She didn't move. She imagined being tackled, then forcibly relieved of her credits and Walker ID. She also imagined wandering around alone, unseen eyes staring her down and following her every movement with hunger.

Layleanna stood and pinned her shoulder bag to her side. She thought about how much safer she would feel following 10 paces behind, gun drawn.

Instead, through the noise of her thoughts, she politely inclined her head and followed.

"How much longer? I can't keep up with you."

The dark figure turned, giving her a quizzical look.

A man, she thought.

Their black combat boots looked practical given the terrain, while Layleanna was left picking carefully around strewn concrete and haphazardly-piled debris. She knew hurricanes wracked the city on occasion, but she never realized how bad they hit. Buildings in the corporate district were repaired within weeks of a hurricane. Buildings in this part of town never seem to find the same funds. Repairs were done by unskilled workers who depended on the property, though many were never done at all.

The figure came toward her at a crushing pace, as jagged chunks of concrete crunched beneath their boots. They now stood so close to her, she wanted to step back but knew she couldn't. The best she could do was lean away to maintain her distance. They bent to scoop her up and carried her through the rubble. The intimacy of this moment revealed to her that this was a woman, clambering with her over the concrete. Her breasts felt soft against Layleanna's thigh. The woman's arms were unnaturally strong for her size.

Augmented, she realized.

The woman quickly put on the distance, reaching the red doorway within minutes. Layleanna felt like a useless fool. It would have taken her all day to reach the same place alone.

"Dad?" the woman called, popping open the red door with her hip. "Dad, I have the corporate chick here."

A man with olive skin and a boxy face came out of the back of the apartment. The right half of his head was shaved and dyed a faded red. He was wearing a white undershirt that clung to his square frame. Both his arms were mech and he had winding lines of Japanese traditional tattoos stretching from his chin, down his throat, to his pecs. They followed the same line the caress of a lover might. Laylanna guessed he was about a half-century old, young and spry.

"Here for the glitch?" Layleanna locked eyes with him and nodded. "Alright, c'mon back. I'll need to put you down."

She followed, again hesitant and terrified. Work on her mech arm had been easier before she had it attached. Now she found she could no longer work on it alone. She needed that extra pair of eyes and hands to manipulate her pieces.

User ukkobiu1998 gestured to an old doctor's table in the middle of his work room. It was a garish turquoise.

"Hop up."

Layleanna inhaled, fully expanding her lungs. With it came the flavor of the room; vinyl, dust, stale hospital, and charged ions from the equipment. She got onto the table.

"Alright, let's look at this bugger." A large overhead lamp rolled itself to him and he adjusted it accordingly. "You said in your DM that it's fritzin' out on you. Is it random? Or do you notice it happening sometimes over others?"

"It used to only be in the middle of the night. I'd wake up and think I'm being hacked again. Now it's random. Little glitches here and there throughout the day where I can't control my arm."

User ukkobiu1998 nodded, his dark brows knit in acknowledgement. He handed Layleanna a plastic mask with a tube. "Put this on and breathe deep, *mi amiga*. I'm gonna knock you out."

Layleanna positioned the mask over her face breathing in quickly. The bright light of the lamp washed out her vision.

"Rise and shine, cupcake."

"What was it?" Layleanna asked sitting up, dazed and groggy. She tentatively tried her left arm.

"Beats the hell out of me. There's nothing mechanically wrong with your arm and I couldn't find any traces of hacking. I did lay a trap, so if it happens again we can take a look. Should get an error code from it, at least." He paused, considering his words. "It might be psychological. You said you've been hacked before, maybe you're anxious and it's glitchin' you out?"

A sharp huff escaped Layleanna. It wasn't something she had considered and now felt it was a logical conclusion. "Thanks for looking into it."

Moments passed between them. A siren wailed as an ambulance rushed across the bridge passing the Sal district by.

"Do you have any Walker cybernetics?" Layleanna asked.

"Not really."

"Well, in the next few weeks keep a close eye on what you have. I've heard something might happen."

User ukkobiu1998 raised a brow, "Thanks for the tip."

Layleanna hopped off the table with the hope she would never have to come back.

Walker Global stood strong as an impenetrable fortress of firewalls and bots. Biding her time was the only weapon she could employ. Acting too soon and asking too many questions would reveal her cause and blow her cover. Each excursion into the system revealed layers of AI, each with a different function to keep the system running. Cleaning up rogue data and pushing it into nearly indecipherable categories; there were hierarchies she wasn't able to see anymore. She tweaked a few pieces of data to see what would happen. Within seconds a bot had corrected her "error" and the data was found again in its proper place.

Damn. Dread rippled through her. Layleanna would have to act fast or she might not be able to escape.

The moment Walker knew they were hacked, she wouldn't be able to leave the building. She had tried logging on remotely but since she didn't have a probable business need for a remote login, she found her access denied. The security at Walker was disheartening.

Layleanna sidestepped the network. It scanned her upon entrance and found legitimate credentials. The interior of the network sprawled out in a black expanse. Once it identified her, the bot moved on to other tasks. She created her work space as she usually did, calling up a window and boxing herself into a soon-to-be new space on the network. She could feel the bots buzzing past periodically scanning her code, almost interjecting and then scuttling along. She would be protected for a short while until her code's purpose became obvious. This of course was the distraction.

When she felt the bots were sufficiently accustomed to her presence, she removed a cable from her arm and hooked directly into the network. Layleanna sucked in a sharp gasp. The system was living! It filled her up in an explosive presence that she felt as warming awe course through her, leaving goosebumps in its wake. She could feel its pulse as it drew data in from across the globe.

The overwhelming feeling subsided and Layleanna was able to make out the images and sensations of that data. She could feel hearts pumping in arrhythmic fashion, the tightening and extension of cybernetic arms. She could see with the unreal clarity of bionic eyes. She heard the cacophony of a billion words being spoken at once. There wasn't the cadence of one particular language, but the noise of a species. She could hear and feel them all in that instant. Then this too subsided and she was able to focus on one thread of information at a time. To Layleanna this was like finding a single molecule of H2O in an ocean.

Swimming through this ocean of knowledge, Layleanna rubbed the sore spot where her mech connected with her arm. Her physical body twitched in response to this action in the digital world. She released Felk. He bloomed in the network, unfurling from a tiny point of light to his digital fuzzy form that she had grown to love. Then he continued to grow and expand. His friendly shaped morphed in a terrifying lizard—almost a dragon— as he reached out into the network; absorbing and assimilating. Years of training would now take its course. Felk knew that not one of Walker Global's cybernetics could continue in their current form. This was a complex task, as each implant had its own function, software that spanned the decades; some even had homegrown firewalls. The sabotage needed to happen en masse so that everyone was too busy putting out the fires. It could easily be weeks before they would be able to address the problem at its core.

A wail of sadness bubbled up and out of Layleanna before she pulled back to detach herself from the buzz of information. She quickly logged off and found herself staring at the water patch on the ceiling above her terminal. A few employees were still logged on. With trembling hands, Layleanna hunched over to gather up her things. She didn't even bother to put her coat on, instead tossing it over her arm.

Get out. Get the fuck out. A chorus. A mantra. *Stay alive and get the fuck out.*

She let the double glass doors to her department slam shut. Her muffled heels ticked too fast against the carpeted hall. The artificial waterfall's rippling sounded sinister and the water smelled stale. Layleanna jammed the button for the elevator and then checked that she had grabbed everything.

Mr. Karumi exited his office a few doors down from the elevator. He locked his door with a wrist swipe and then proceeded to put his coat on while he walked. All the while he kept his eyes locked with Layleanna's.

He knows. The whole building knows, she thought. Her panic pounded wildly in her ears.

"Ms. Graves."

"Mr. Karumi."

The elevator had yet to arrive. Every part of her body was screaming to leave. Layleanna wanted to melt into the floor now that Mr. Karumi stood next to her.

The elevator chimed pleasantly and the doors opened.

Mr. Karumi inclined his head and brought his arm out in a wide swoop. "After you, Ms. Graves."

She obliged. He pressed the button for the lobby, not even inquiring as to if that was where she was headed. His assumption was correct.

Layleanna's tight tummy flip indicated their descent. She ran a selection of lobby scenarios through her head. She knew she had seconds to decide her next move. Before she could consider anymore, her left hand seized.

"No!"

"Pardon?" Mr. Kumari asked, his mouth open to say something more, but instead he choked. His hand flew to his chest and he doubled over.

Layleanna couldn't control her arm. Sparks of electricity arched through her synth-skin. Her fingers spasmed: open-shut, open-shut. Nothing she did could stop it. Then it wrenched at the elbow. She clutched it with her right hand, preventing it from grabbing her face or throat.

Layleanna screamed.

The elevator stopped at the lobby, chiming politely

and opening its doors. Another employee leaving for the day saw them askew in the elevator as the doors began to close.

She had fallen backward and the rail bit into her ribs. Layleanna watched helpless as the man raced toward them. His eyebrows framed his eyes, damp with fear. Below was the wide O of his mouth; the single dot of what appeared to be a double exclamation point. He couldn't hear their screaming, though, as his cochlear implant had cut out. But he could see pain painted across their bodies.

A primal yell escaped him. The formation of the sound was somehow accented without the auditory feedback of his voice.

* * *

Layleanna woke up in the lobby to the sounds of rapid speech. Beneath that she heard the popping of gunshots. They were far away, outside maybe?

She also noticed how oppressively humid it was inside the building. It had never been less than a crisp and comfortable 70F at Walker. The air wrapped around her like a down comforter. The lobby tile beneath her was warm to the touch. Layleanna sat up.

She watched as paramedics and an EMT bot loaded Mr. Karumi onto a stretcher. The bot was pumping air into him through a mask attachment. Mr Karumi's fingers were blue and his face sheened with sweat.

Her left arm was seized but she could function without it. More employees were being examined by EMTs. A woman she recognized from User Experience sat at the rim of the now-defunct waterfall. Her normally immaculate hair was mused and she had a scrape on her forehead. An EMT was gently pressing his fingers into her throat and lymph nodes, checking for trauma. She turned her head from side to side and then as though the whole exchange were awkward she let out a shrill laugh. Layleanna could tell they were on edge.

The popping from outside increased. Layleanna realized that the gangs would have spread out from the Sal and Honomi districts. The souped-up cyber psychotics would be at the front of the invasion. She hadn't considered those most likely to use Omni products would be the cyber psychotics and they would be unaffected by the hacking. This wasn't like the Board of Directors said it would be like at all. This wasn't about some moral high ground to free the humans from the machines. It was about market share. With Walker devastated as a corporation and their reputation shattered, consumers would have no choice but to turn to Omni. At this realization, Layleanna clenched her fist and saw red push in at the edges of her vision.

She watched, as though from a great distance, the battle ragging outside. Walker Security, having been decreased greatly in number from the hack, was trying to keep the gangs at bay. Their chaotic movement and speed were an advantage against the security team. Layleanna guessed there was no one to call for backup since all of the districts would be experiencing the same level of violence. The fact EMTs were here at all meant they were close or already on site before the attack.

Layleanna reached for her gun and exited through the front door. This time she surveyed the melee from the opposite side of safety. Of the ten people exchanging fire, she appraised that two were cyber psychotics. Their unpredictability was the true threat. Without crouching or otherwise concealing her presence she set her sight on the most crazed. Half his face was mech as well as his gun arm.

Classy, she thought. *All the better to shoot you with my dear.* The top of his bald head was red and peeling from exposure and his precious Zohai. His eyes darted frantically and where they roamed, so did his fire. Layleanna aimed for those crazed eyes and shot. He crumpled—lifeless—

and her distance spared her the crack of his mech hitting pavement.

Next to him stood a wiry individual. This hothead was one upgrade away from a cyborg and too meched out to discern a gender. Their gaze shifted to Layleanna as she was the source of the last cyber psychotic going down. She felt something sting in her left shoulder, then she heard a bullet ping off her frozen arm. Time felt as slow as honey pouring into tea. Layleanna pivoted slightly, then fired two rapid shots at the transhuman. While she knew her shots found their mark, they were unphased and began advancing on her. She fired more, but knew her round was almost up. She took cover rolling behind a fallen pylon. The transhuman began moving toward her. Walker Security took advantage of her ambush and shot down two more gang members while the transhuman went after her.

Layleanna popped back up from behind her cover, blood rushing from her shoulder, to take the hothead. Having advanced at an incredible rate, they were already within arm's reach. Layleanna fired desperately at them, but her gun clicked uselessly. Security had turned their sights to them now and a rain of bullets pelleted the hothead's body. Many ricocheted, but enough found their mark. The transhuman, too, crumpled to the concrete before Walker's headquarters.

* * *

Layleanna returned home for the first time since she installed Felk on the network. She guessed it had been nearly 24 hours since Walker's network and cybernetics went down, but she couldn't be sure. Her internet connection had gone down with the hack.

Walker stocks were in freefall. They had yet to find a bottom as more reports across the world came in about Walker devices failing. Sex bots in Thailand were glitching out; pacemakers in Spain failed, one killing the President;

whole limbs moved of their own volition. Walker Global's name was sneered at internationally and across media outlets.

"Welcome home, Ms. Graves," her assistant greeted, its artificial voice pleasant, but flat.

Layleanna didn't acknowledge the bot. She was bone weary from the adrenalin and chaos. But exhaustion propelled her to seek refuge in the tightly-monitored walls of her apartment. Arc had become a warzone in a matter of hours and she was no longer safe outside.

Layleanna bent to take off her shoes, struggling with the straps. Her feet were swollen from her stumbling walk through town, and the exposed skin was tender to the touch. Cyber psychotics had jacked most the coaches and she was unable to get a ride. Bitterness welled up in her, followed closely by pride.

I did it.

"Did you have a good day at work, Ms. Graves?"

Why did this stupid bot insist on engaging her in idle conversation? She had made it clear in the settings she wanted nothing to do with it.

She had brought down Walker Global as Omni's Board of Directors had instructed, *Infiltrate Walker and invade their impenetrable firewalls to free humanity from merging with the machines.*

What a fat fucking lie, she snorted.

Being careful not to catch her tender, sunburned skin on the edges of the kitchen cabinets, Layleanna reached up to the cupboard and pulled down a glass. She held it under the dispenser expectantly.

"Would you like some water?"

She rolled her eyes. "Yes, what a sensible suggestion."

But at least the mission had been accomplished, even if she felt used by it. It was about market shares, not the greater good… the bastards.

She brought the glass from the dispenser to her lips.

Exhaustion clouded her sense. She should have noticed the delicate carbonation in her glass or the tangy, sour flavor. She was several gulps in when her throat burned intensely. It was as though her throat and lungs were as seized as her arm.

Attempting to inhale, she clutched at her throat, then her chest. A light-headed feeling made her dizzy and she stumbled to the counter. Her ears buzzed loudly, choking out the sound of her gasping for air.

Layleanna wanted to say something. To ask the ridiculous bot if it could call for medical help or even security. Someone. All she could manage was to slap the counter repeatedly as though this would help her draw air into her burning lungs.

Minutes passed. She sunk to the floor, her face turning a horrid shade of purple. Blackness seeped in at the edges of her vision. There was no one.

Sprawled on the kitchen floor where she had collapsed, Layleanna did not move again.

"Mr. Karumi, I am happy to report—the traitor is dead."

SCARLET II

By Todd Cinani.

Scarlet sat in an uncomfortable chair on the wrong side of a glass desk. The glass projected random images of people wanted for one crime or another. She was wondering if she'd see herself, or if there was no need because she'd already been picked up. As she was waiting for the detective, she called Beetle. His face, happy, no longer worried, popped into her heads-up display.

"Hey Scar. How's business?" Beetle asked relaxed.

"Not great. I'm at the station."

"Yeah, what station?"

"The train station," she responded sarcastically. "I'm at the fucking police station."

"Oh shit, well leave us out of it, will ya?" His eyes were wide.

"Relax, you're not involved," she sighed. "I just need to find Chris. You know how to reach him?"

"Not likely. He's in the network now."

"What do you mean?"

"He fucked off and decided to live in the network. His body is holed up somewhere hooked up to whatever keeps him alive, but his mind is a hundred percent in the net. No one has seen him in ages."

"Great. Well, see if you can get a hold of his net self." The detective was returning to the desk with a cup of coffee. "Look I gotta go now."

"Wait, Scar, he doesn't respo…" She cut him off.

"So Scarlet, is it?" the detective asked suspiciously. "No last name?"

"Not that I remember. I was raised in the lower levels. We don't much need last names down there because so few survive to twenty."

"Hmm, you seem to have done well for yourself."

"And I clawed and bit for every inch I rose. What's your point?"

"I'm suggesting you must have been involved in crime to make it this far up."

"Some, but once I went legit, I stopped all that."

"You make enough money legitimately to live where you do and have that nice bike forensics are going over?"

"Yes. I have some very wealthy corporate clients who don't want their purchases made public so they hire me to be discrete." Scarlet added. "They won't find anything, you know. The forensics team I mean."

"And why is that?" the detective asked.

"Because I never picked up the damn thing."

"Walker says you did. They cannot find it and you were the only anomaly in their day-to-day."

"Unless they guy who jumped on the back of the bike had it, I can't help you. As soon as I got there all hell broke loose. Their security was shooting at us, the guy jumped on the bike and I got the fuck out of there," Scarlet explained.

"Where is this *guy* now?"

"Go about hundred yards east of the tower, then go all the way down to the floor. There won't be much more than a stain left but maybe your box hasn't been picked up by one of the unfortunates yet."

"And who hired you for this job?"

"Look, I already told you guys, Joseph Souz hired me. The man himself."

"This man hired you?" The detective threw up an image of an elderly man with a thin hairline.

"Of course not, and anyway there are no images of Souz. Nobody knows what he looks like except maybe me and his direct coworkers and superiors."

"We know what he looks like." The detective smirked.

"Yeah. Like this?" Scarlet threw up the bio Souz had given her last night. "That is the real Joseph Souz."

"Unfortunately that has to be as fake as your legitimate courier jobs." The confident sarcasm took her aback. She had a feeling there may be issues with the bio on Souz, that it may be fake. But C500k, well, risk versus reward.

"How do you know your guy is Souz and not mine?" Scarlet asked, a little less sure of herself.

"Walker released his file once Souz was found dead on his office floor. Looks like a heart attack but probably poison." The detective was gathering up some glass rectangles full of data. "From what I've seen, if you have a body, looks like a heart attack, and there is a glass of tea or something nearby it's always poison."

"When did it happen?" She asked calmly.

"Yesterday afternoon, a few hours before you met our dead man." He gave her a serious look. "If you are not involved you better go into hiding. If you are, you probably won't be around much longer." He turned and started to walk away.

"Oh and by the way, your bike cleared inspection, you are free to go," he added, not bothering to look back.

Involved. She sure as hell was involved. She had the fucking thing people were killing each other over in her damn bike. Scarlet decided it would stay there for now. If the police scan didn't see it, no one else would either. But then maybe they did see it, and were planning to use her as bait, to follow her to get to the bad guys. All she knew was she needed to get the fuck out of Dodge. She'd go straight home, drink a bottle or two, and try to figure this out. Or at least figure out her next move.

* * *

Scarlet met Beetle at one of the many noodle shops that scatter on the levels. They, or rather more particularly she, needed a way to contact Chris if she was going to figure out what the hell was going on. Chris was the best NetFlyer around, and just happened to be the only one she knew with any talent. Didn't hurt that they had a thing once.

"So how do we get a hold of him?" Scarlet asked.

"Well, like I said, he's not on the line. Doesn't respond to messages and the like. You've gotta entice him."

"How?"

"You hide a message in one of the communications he follows. Preferably a group or business the he has a problem with, but it can't be obvious. Everyone has some problem with the major corps, yeah? You have to go smaller, more obscure, almost random."

"Like…?" Scarlet was starting to get slightly frustrated. Why tell her all this? She just needed an answer now.

"Like Tessa Sushi." Beetle leaned back, raising his arms in a "tah-dah!" expression.

"What?"

"Tessa Sushi. Chris has been waging a mild net war with them for months. Changing their coupons, messing with their reviews, and whatnot."

"Why a sushi joint?" She was not impressed. "Seems a little trivial"

"That is the brilliance of it. It's small, random, exactly the thing that will catch his big brain's attention."

"But why is he so hung up on this sushi place?" At this point she was just curious, but her question wasn't really relevant and she knew that.

"Fuck if I know. Maybe they gave him crap that made him sick, the bill was too big, don't know. But it must have been when he was walking around, not hooked up to machines."

"Okay, so send him something simple hacked into their ads. Something like 'Scarlet is looking for you' or even better 'needs you'. That may get his attention."

"Done. And what are you going to pay me for this hack job?"

"Ever-lasting friendship."

"Great, pro bono, yeah?" Beetle responded, a little snarky.

Scarlet gave him a kiss on the head and paid for their noodles before leaving.

* * *

Scarlet sat below her big round window in her comfy chair with Fenris at her feet. She was going through the daily job roster to see if anything interesting came up. Something that paid anyway. The hot jobs seemed to have dried up a bit since her little run in with the cops. Folks always got nervous when you got pulled into the station, thinking you may not be so discrete anymore. She might have to wait until someone got desperate, or Beetle came up with something. For now, she was sipping synth bourbon, scrolling through the legit jobs for something. She probably needed one anyway, to keep the license up to code.

"Hello Scarlet. You need something?" The voice, uninvited, just popped into her head and startled her. She jerked upright, some of the bourbon sloshing out of the glass onto Fenris' head. He looked up at her, nonplussed.

"Chris...?" She asked unsure.

"Yes."

"Jesus! Christopher, you can bypass node firewall now?"

"Only to communicate. I can't make you dance like a puppet or anything."

"Where are you?"

"Everywhere, anywhere. I have the city and everything in it at my fingertips."

"Okay, that must be mind-bending. But I mean, where physically are you? I need you to look at something."

"Physically, I am of no consequence. What you hear is what you get." Chris' voice sounded slightly sad at this, but only slightly. "So you seem to be in some trouble with Walker Global."

"You know?"

"The net knows, therefore I know," he responded flatly. "Your escape from the tower was quite thrilling."

"Yeah, you can say that. Look, I need to see you in person."

"You won't like what you see. Better this way."

"I need to show you what I have so you can help me figure out what the fuck is going on."

"Fuck, it's one of those." His voice turned a bit annoyed.

"One of what?" She could sense something not right with her node. He had hacked her.

"Put your armor on."

"What?" At this point she was speaking aloud. Fenris' ears pricked, and he went to the door. It opened and he looked back at her before charging off down the hall. "What the fuck! Fen!" The door closed.

"Armor now, please." Chris' voice was slightly impatient. "Fenris is fine. I sent him away to avoid harm."

"Avoid what?" She was attaching the armor.

"There are several heavily armed and armored personnel taking elevators to your floor. Jesus, Scarlet, your security here is really for shit. Tisk-tisk."

"So I didn't want cannons in the ceiling. And Fenris is usually enough when he's not sent off." Scarlet could feel anger surging, and tried not to target Chris with it.

"Not enough for what's coming. They are exiting the elevators. Is the box still in the bike?"

"Bike? Yes, how did you know?"

"I've been accessing your memory log. I'm not an idiot."

"Oh, but isn't that..."

"The bike is waiting outside. Go through the window now."

"Really?" Her helmet was closing over her head and the gun popped into her hand from her thigh. "But I like that window," she said under her breath as she shot it out and leapt through. She was in a free fall for a couple seconds, until the bike rose up to meet her. She secured herself and sped off.

"So the good news is Fenris is alive and well, and you'll get to see what is left of the physical me. It's the only truly safe place." Chris told her. "Your bike has the destination plugged in."

"Thanks." There was an explosion behind her, as her apartment burst fire from the windows. "Christ, thanks. I miss you Chris. I..."

"I'll leave you for now Scarlet," he sighed. "I'll connect again later at... well, where I am."

* * *

Scarlet had the bike, and the bike had the box. The destination icon blipped on the edge of the Arc boundary. She needed a drink first, or several, so she sped off to a nearby dive she frequented. She knew the people and they would protect her. She pulled the bike around to the delivery dock and hopped off to go to the front. As she walked in the bartender and patrons all looked up at her before going back to their business. Tre, the bartender, smiled and pulled a bottle down from the shelf behind the bar.

"Hey, Scarlet," he greeted her. "Been a while."

"It's been a week, Tre."

"A week is a long time without your red radiance." Tre flirted as he usually did, but she knew his interests lay elsewhere. Tre set the bottle and a glass down before her.

"It's been a week." Scarlet said with feigned exhaustion.

"Sounds rough. Do tell."

"In the last hour or so an old boyfriend popped into my head, my dog, wolf actually, ran away and some assholes blew up my apartment."

"I heard there was a note out on you. Didn't believe it, though." Tre whispered across the bar.

"You hear who's holding it?" Scarlet whispered back.

"Some corporate guys. Walker Global I think." His eyes darted about the bar. "It's a big note, Scarlet, even some of your friends may take it."

"Thanks for the warning, Tre." She poured the glass full and downed it. "Guess I should pay off my tab?"

"That would be generous of you," Tre responded with a sad smile.

Scarlet sent him the credits for two years' worth of drinking and walked out. Back on the bike she decided to go to Chris' place. She let the bike drive while she scrolled through her ever-dwindling contacts list. Some remained loyal, some left and several, she believed, still followed in case they could collect on the note.

The bike cruised between the towers, which had become fewer and further between. The closer they got to the northern Fringe, the more run-down Arc became, and the shorter the buildings got. The older parts of the city were like this, not much more than a ruined monument to what had come before. Most of the cityscape was dark. This part of town was the dead zone. Few lived here because it lacked the basic amenities and infrastructure which were dedicated to the new city. There were only the shadiest people, those who didn't want to be found but couldn't make the leap to the Fringe yet; people like Chris.

Looking at the map in her ocular Heads Up, she could see that he must reside in an old luxury condo building. Taking back control of the bike, Scarlet flew it down into the atrium, the glass roof long since gone. She guided her bike over to a walkway that looked over the Atrium, with its broken chandeliers and fountain bottom. The bike nestled into the rotting carpet of the walkway.

Hopping off the bike she checked the signal. Chris was close, just a few doors away. She felt anxious, partly to see him again but mostly to see what he had become. She knew that in some not small way she was the reason he had retreated into the digital world. A pit grew in her stomach.

"You must be Scarlet," a deep voice rose from the darkness to say. Scarlet spun toward the voice, trying to peer into the shadows. Her hand instinctively went to her hip, but she stopped short of releasing her gun.

"I don't mean you any harm," the voice said, calming, as a tall figure limped out of the darkness. Enhancing her vision slightly, Scarlet saw that he was a dark-skinned man with long curly hair. He wore homemade armor which looked like it was from another time, with a metal leg you could barely call cybernetic. He also carried an old rifle that looked like it fired self-propelled rounds. "I'm here to take you to Chris."

"And you are?" Scarlet asked carefully.

"For lack of a better word, his servant. I keep him alive, and he pays me handsomely for it. I'm Andre."

Chris' bodyguard and servant led Scarlet down a series of stairways and halls that let to other stairways and halls. It was much further away from the actual beacon Chris had provided than Scarlet would have expected.

"Hey, Andre, why so far?"

"Although you are his friend, no one really trusts anyone anymore. Who's to say you don't land with a squad? My advice, actually."

Sad state of affairs, Scarlet thought. After all, she broadcast her arrival to Chris as soon as she entered the atrium. But maybe she brought more with her than she realized. There were people trying to kill her. Eventually they reached the door of the condo that housed Chris. Andre let Scarlet in first. She walked into a living room that would have been the height of fashion decades ago. It was mostly undisturbed, only dust on table chairs and everything else. It had a great view of the now-dead cityscape. Chris was over in a massive chair which made his wizened, hairless body look frailer than she thought possible for a living person. He was not much more than tight skin stretched over bones. It made Scarlet want to retch. "Chris…" She repressed a gag. "What the fuck…"

"It is only the body. The mind is well and working fine," Chris responded through speakers in the walls.

Such a waste, she thought. *What did you do?* The words kept running through her mind like a mantra. "But the cost…" she uttered.

"I know it's worrying, and it's something I have been trying to address. I am mostly digital but there seems to be no way to make the final leap. When my body dies, so does my digital life, because it is all tied to my living brain. Once the brain goes, so does everything else." Chris threw up an old holo zombie movie, and a character's voice floats through the room. "Shoot them in the head. Once the brain goes, they are dead. You have to shoot them in the head."

"Jesus, Chris…"

"Well, without a bit of humor what have you got? Was a good film actually." The speakers responded with some static. Andre moved to one of the control panels and made adjustments.

"Your bags need to be changed, boss." Andre said over his shoulder. "Mind if I take care of that?"

"No, by all means, commence. She has seen the worst."

Scarlet had not. She was not prepared for the sacks of waste being removed from the back of the chair. *This is worse than death*, she thought. Who cares if he lived in the net fantasy, if he had to have someone change his shit bags? She would choose her death, and it would be nothing like this. Part of her wished she'd been caught unawares by the corporate kill team and everything ended quickly.

"It's good to see you again, Scarlet. With my own eyes that is. You have not changed a bit." *You sure as hell have*, she thought. His own eyes were moist globs poking out of a drawn skull. Where was the blond, blue-eyed boy she fell for? The sculpted body she explored with her fingers and tongue. Lost, all but dead. "Good...to see you too...Chris," she tried.

"Nonsense. I am nothing more than a poor battery that fuels a much greater self," the walls spoke. "By the way, I think I figured out some of your current problem. Walker Global never hired you to transport their research. It was supposed to be kept in-house. However, a very secret anti-cyber group had killed Souz and arranged for the theft of the data cube. Once it was stolen, they needed to get it far away from Walker, which was where you came in. By all accounts, the man who received the data cube from Souz both killed him and stole the prize."

"What is it?" Scarlet asked.

"Don't know. Important. Do you have it with you?"

Scarlet hesitated at first, but then reluctantly offered, "Yes, I have it here." She had taken it out of the bike on the journey to this condo city, and pulled it out of her pocket.

"Good. Andre, would you be so kind as to take it and place it in device thirteen?"

"In, sir, door closed." Andre had taken the box from Scarlet, and placed it in something that looked like an old microwave.

"Huh, shielded well…well, indeed. I cannot really analyze it, but I can get some snippets of what it is for. My opinion is that it should be returned to Walker ASAP. Do not give it to the group who hired you, or something very valuable to us all may be lost."

"So what the fuck is it? And how do I give it back without getting killed?"

"It may just be immortality for a price. But you know how all good tech goes. The price comes down as others steal the data." Chris responded. "As far as not getting killed, I am arranging a meeting. It will be a bit of a stand-off, so be prepared for the worst. I'll send Andre with you."

"Oh, fuck," came the response from both Scarlet and Andre, though Andre added a few more well-chosen words.

* * *

The meeting would be between Scarlet and representatives from Walker Global, in order to return what was stolen from them. On their part, they would close the police investigation and remove their note for her. They would meet on a long sky bridge in Chris's desolate part of town. Andre would be hidden on one of the nearby towers as a backup sniper. Hopefully things would go according to plan, but Scarlet would take a small hit of Event Horizon to sharpen her instincts and combat skills. Chris had loaded a group of new military-grade combat skills into her node. With the combined drugs and skills, she'd become a slaughter goddess. The idea was no violence and a simple hand-off, but if everything went balls up they'd be in a better situation than their opponents would expect.

Scarlet and Andre flew on her bike towards the bridge, dropping Andre at his post. Scarlet landed the bike near the center of the bridge. She was early on purpose. Getting off the bike, she sat cross-legged on the bridge, facing the direction Walker was supposed to arrive from. The bridge was fairly wide, around ten meters across, so there was plenty of room to move about if needed. Andre signaled incoming and Scarlet rose from her crouching position. She turned her armor's setting to active, including her back unit which she rarely used. It drained the suit batteries and power, but it could release holy hell. It could also send forth nano-bots to repair her or her suit. Only the best for Scarlet...

An air transport hovered into view and landed on the far side of the bridge across from Scarlet. She hadn't yet injected the EH yet. She'd wait until she knew how things would play out first. Her eyes enhanced the image across the bridge, and she could see a group of heavily armed and armored figures approaching. There was a svelte woman in a classy business suit, also no doubt armored to a degree, in the lead of the hulking figures. The woman gave Scarlet some relief. Not that women were any less ruthless and bloodthirsty than men, but they were also a great deal more rational than men. The guns were not an assassin team, but her protection. That played in Scarlet's favor. They were actually here to make a deal, not just wreak retribution. Chris must have negotiated well.

Scarlet watched and thought as they approached, until they were twenty meters away and stopped. If they wanted her dead, they would have already started shooting.

"Hi!" Scarlet chirped, for lack of a better introduction. "I think there's been some confusion here."

"You stole something very important from us, seems pretty cut and dried," the woman responded.

"Well, not quite stole actually," Scarlet defended. "I was hired by your Dr. Souz to transport sensitive information from your tower to another location. Not uncommon in my line of work."

"That was not Dr. Souz. You had an inside engineer help you steal it, and you ran," the woman responded again, cold as a snake.

"Yes, it turns out he was a fraud, Dr. Souz, but he had all the proper credentials, and since you guys hid the appearance of the real Dr. Souz, who's to say who it was? And yes, I did get suspicious when your guards started shooting at the engineer, but I really, until now, haven't had the time to figure it all out with the cops harassing me and your death squad blowing up my apartment."

"I'm sorry it has been difficult for you," the woman replied sarcastically. "We would have reached you immediately, if we were not dealing with the death of our lead engineer in all projects, not to mention the theft of our greatest discovery."

"Who killed Souz? The real one…"

"It was the engineer who stole the data cube and tried to escape with you," the woman offered. "Now, if you would be so kind, the data cube?" She then asked, with her hand outstretched.

So far, so good, Scarlet thought as she retrieved the silver cube from her bike. Just a bit of a walk over to the Walker line, and hopefully it would be over. "Scarlet, another incoming to the tower behind you. Sorry, just noticed their landing, I was concentrated on the Walker group before you." Andre's voice posted in her head.

"More Walker?" Scarlet messaged back.

"I don't know, but they came in stealthily."

Scarlet, cube in hand, turned back toward the woman and the Walker group. "Did you send a second team?"

"No…" the woman's face fell slightly. She was telling the truth.

"Then this situation is about to get interesting," Scarlet replied, looking down at the cube in her palm. *Screw it,* she thought, and raised her hand to toss it at the Walker group.

"I would not do that if I were you," a great voice came from behind Scarlet. The Walker group had already seen the incoming force of independent paramilitary crossing the bridge, and took defensive positions with the woman moving between them back towards her vehicle. Scarlet looked back and forth between the two groups. The imposter Souz was leading the paramilitary group, which had less armor than the Walker goons, but outnumbered them. "Andre, when it hits the fan, target the rebels, not Walker," Scarlet signaled.

"Hey, lady!" Scarlet shouted in the direction of Walker Global. "Catch!" She tossed the data cube as far as she could. The woman had turned around, and as she dove forward to catch the cube, chaos erupted.

Scarlet felt the EH course through her blood and drive to her node. After that, it was all instinct. A blur of violence as she met the rebels face on. Blades and bullets flying into and slashing through the enemy's armor. A blood mist everywhere. She had no control over nor did she even care about what would happen to her, a perfect creature, a goddess of war. Mini-missiles flew from her rear pack, and as the blasts from the hand cannons tore at her armor, hoards of nano-bots burst forth to repair it like ants on speed. Spinning and weaving with nothing but quick, harsh death emitting from her, she watched from far away, as if it were all a film. For an instant, from that safe distance, she saw the imposter Souz's head between her hands, before it was crushed into a paste of bone and blood.

The battle seemed to end as fast as it began, except on this side she found herself prone upon a pile of bodies. She opened her eyes to Andre standing over her, a look of sadness on his face as he reached out an arm to help her up. The rebels dead. What was left of Walker fled. It was over, for now at least.

* * *

Scarlet sat on the hole where her wall used to be, looking out over the cityscape. It was a fairly clear day and the sun was out, a beautiful day for Arc. Fenris had come back, and was panting next to her. She dangled her feet over the edge, with thousands of meters of nothing below them.

The sound of the android's steps crunching on debris as it entered the apartment pricked up Fenris' ears. He turned toward the sound, giving a low growl as the android looked about.

"Is everything good?" Scarlet asked, without turning.

The android approached and sat down on the edge of the hole next to her. She turned then, and took in a rubbery-looking human analog with a projection of Chris's face on the front of its head. "Good so far. This is just a trial prototype," it said in Chris' voice.

"I meant with me," Scarlet snapped.

"Oh... Yes, everything is fine. The rebels are demoralized and scattering as Walker places notes on anyone they find. Walker have dropped their note on you, and the police don't care about you if Walker doesn't," Chris explained via the android. "This whole thing may have actually increased your rep."

"When the jobs start rolling in, I'll let you know."

"They will," Chris reassured.

"This was all down to you, wasn't it?" Scarlet asked knowing the answer.

"What do you mean?"

"Your body was dying, well dead now, and you needed another one." She tossed a pebble-sized piece of her wall over the side. "Then you hear Walker Global is making a system that will transport a human mind into a new body. Not just a copy of the mind, but the actual consciousness. True immortality, if you don't mind living in that." She looked directly into the android's face for the first time since it arrived.

"It's a protot..."

"Prototype. Yes, I know. You find a way to live onward, but you also find out that this subversive group wants to destroy the tech, and Dr. Souz has the only engineering specs so they bribe his assistant. Knowing this would happen quickly, you arrange for these rebels to get my information and hire me. I do the job, but you alert Walker and suddenly everyone is after me."

"Well I…"

"On the run and confused you make a bet, knowing me and my dwindling list of friends, that I will reach out to you for help. Good job on that."

Scarlet tossed another wall pebble into the mist below. Chris is silent, the projection of his face looking melancholy.

"So I come and you arrange an elaborate showdown with Walker so I can return the tech to them and you get a body. But, being a dick, you also invite the rebels to the party almost getting me killed. I was just your puppet in all this."

"The rebels had to show up so Walker would think you were duped in to all this. Got conned by a criminal outfit and just trying to make things right. I'm sorry, Scarlet. I was dying and I needed someone…"

"Prototype, huh? Should've waited for the full model," she said, benign, as she pushed the android over the side. Fenris looked down, watching the fall begin, and issued a curious whine. Chris screamed with his electronic larynx, as it plummeted down into the mist and disappeared.

Yes, it was a beautiful day for Arc.

PLAYLIST

Scarlet by Todd Cinani
- "Funk Ad" by Daft Punk.
- "Long & Lost" by Florence + The Machine.
- "Is This The End" by Joseph William Morgan.

Midnight on the Midway by J. L. Aarne
- "City of Ghosts" by Crockett.
- "Flesh and Bone" by Black Math.
- "Colorful Mind" by Broken Iris.

Broadcast 2220 by Davene Le Grange
- "Razors Edge" by Digital Daggers.
- "Don't Speak" by Hidden Citizens, Tim Halperin.
- "Soldier" by Firewoodisland.

Neo(N) Bushido by Patrick Tillett
- "Novocaine" by Hidden Citizens, Tim Halperin.
- "Ghostblade" by MythFox.
- "Chosen" by Generdyn, Svrcina.

Getting Clean by Max McCamish
- "Lotus Land" by Philter.

- "Malicious Hardware" by Ex Machina, Ogre.
- "Through the Eyes of a Child" by AURORA.

Layers (Taylor will mess you up and eat your soul) by Tracy Cross
- "Cyberpunk" by Max Brhon.
- "Satisfy" by NERO.
- "Animal" by Chase Holfelder.
- "French Kiss" by Lil Louis.

Regret Me Not by Ava Silurian
- "Willow Tree" by Twin Wild.
- "Every Breath You Take" by Chase Holfelder.
- "Dreamweaver" by J2, Keeley Bumford.

Felk the Network by Amber Benbow
- "Underground" by Lindsey Stirling.
- "Call of Destiny" by Josh Kramer.
- "Twisted" by MISSIO.

Scarlet II by Todd Cinani
- "Warfare" by Katie Garfield.
- "Immortalized" by Hidden Citizens, Keeley Bumford.
- "Your World Will Fail" by Les Friction.

Prester John
By Richard Denham

He sits on his jewelled throne on the Horn of Africa in the maps of the sixteenth century. He can see his whole empire reflected in a mirror outside his palace. He carries three crosses into battle and each cross is guarded by one hundred thousand men. He was with St Thomas in the third century when he set up a Christian church in India. He came like a thunderbolt out of the far East eight centuries later, to rescue the crusaders clinging on to Jerusalem. And he was still there when Portuguese explorers went looking for him in the fifteenth century.

He went by different names. The priest who was also a king was Ong Khan; he was Genghis Khan; he was Lebna Dengel. Above all, he was a Christian king who ruled a vast empire full of magical wonders: men with faces in their chests; men with huge, backward-facing feet; rivers and seas made of sand. His lands lay next to the earthly Paradise which had once been the Garden of Eden. He wrote letters to popes and princes. He promised salvation and hope to generations.

But it was noticeable that as men looked outward, exploring more of the natural world; as science replaced superstition and the age of miracles faded, Prester John was always elsewhere. He was beyond the Mountains of the Moon, at the edge of the earth, near the mouth of Hell.

Was he real? Did he ever exist? This book will take you on a journey of a lifetime, to worlds that might have been, but never were. It will take you, if you are brave enough, into the world of Prester John.

The Ones That Got Away
By Lisa Hill

Have you ever had that feeling that you just needed to escape? Runaway from life, from all its problems; **be the one that got away?**

Tilly Henshaw has. Tilly wants to escape. Escape her suffocating mum, her dementing gran and finally shake off the stigmatism attached to ADHD; a condition she was diagnosed with when she was fourteen.

When the opportunity arises to escape to the sleepy, Cornish fishing village of Hope Cove, Tilly grabs it with both hands. But she soon discovers that she's not the only one who's runaway to Cornwall and everyone's keeping their reasons for escaping firmly to themselves.

As Tilly starts uncovering family secrets, she begins to understand there is no running away from your problems; you can't build a hopeful future without confronting who and what hurt you in your past.

Sirkkusaga
By Kyt Wright

A saga − a long story of heroic achievement, especially a medieval prose narrative in Old Norse or a long, involved story, account, or series of incidents often named for the principal character.

Several hundred years after an world-shattering war, two of the surviving nations, the Reignweald and the Dominion have fought themselves to a standstill, both remaining determined to control of what's left of it.

Sirki Vigsdottir, a songstress who performs under the name Freya in folk-rock group *The Harvest* is beautiful, self-centered woman who is fond of drink and a recovering addict to boot, not the sort of girl a boy brings home to mother.

Following an attack from an unexpected quarter, abilities awaken within Sirki, who begins a journey of self-discovery. These new found skills attract the attention of both the Psi, a mysterious group of telepaths headed by the fearsome Mina and an equally sinister government department; the ACG.

As it becomes clear that her life of self-indulgence is over, Sirki wonders if her new-found powers are a blessing or a curse.

Arthur: Shadow of a God
By Richard Denham

King Arthur has fascinated the Western world for over a thousand years and yet we still know nothing more about him now than we did then. Layer upon layer of heroics and exploits has been piled upon him to the point where history, legend and myth have become hopelessly entangled.

In recent years, there has been a sort of scholarly consensus that 'the once and future king' was clearly some sort of Romano-British warlord, heroically stemming the tide of wave after wave of Saxon invaders after the end of Roman rule. But surprisingly, and no matter how much we enjoy this narrative, there is actually next-to-nothing solid to support this theory except the wishful thinking of understandably bitter contemporaries. The sources and scholarship used to support the 'real Arthur' are as much tentative guesswork and pushing 'evidence' to the extreme to fit in with this version as anything involving magic swords, wizards and dragons. Even Archaeology remains silent. Arthur is, and always has been, the square peg that refuses to fit neatly into the historians round hole.

Arthur: Shadow of a God gives a fascinating overview of Britain's lost hero and casts a light over an often-overlooked and somewhat inconvenient truth; Arthur was almost certainly not a man at all, but a god. He is linked inextricably to the world of Celtic folklore and Druidic traditions. Whereas tyrants like Nero and Caligula were men who fancied themselves gods; is it not possible that Arthur was a god we have turned into a man? Perhaps then there is a truth here. Arthur, 'The King under the Mountain'; sleeping until his return will never return, after all, because he doesn't need to. Arthur the god never left in the first place and remains as popular today as he ever was. His legend echoes in stories, films and games that are every bit as imaginative and fanciful as that which the minds of talented bards such as Taliesin and Aneirin came up with when the mists of the 'dark ages' still swirled over Britain – and perhaps that is a good thing after all, most at home in the imaginations of children and adults alike – being the Arthur his believers want him to be.

A Storm of Magic
By Ashley Laino

Being brought back from the dead is an impressive trick, even for magician Darien Burron. Now he must try and use his sleight of hand to swindle modern-day witch, Mirah, to sign her power away, or end up a tormented demon in the afterlife.

Meanwhile, sixteen-year-old Mirah is starting to lose control of her powers. After an incident at her aunt's Witchery store, Mirah is sent to a secret coven to learn to control her abilities. While away, Mirah meets up with a soft-spoken clairvoyant, a brazen storm witch, and the creator of dark magic itself. The young woman must learn to trust in herself before she loses herself entirely to the darkness that hunts her.

Weirder War Two
By Richard Denham & Michael Jecks

Did a Warner Bros. cartoon prophesize the use of the atom bomb? Did the Allies really plan to use stink bombs on the enemy? Why did the Nazis make their own version of Titanic and why were polar bear photographs appearing throughout Europe?

The Second World War was the bloodiest of all wars. Mass armies of men trudged, flew or rode from battlefields as far away as North Africa to central Europe, from India to Burma, from the Philippines to the borders of Japan. It saw the first aircraft carrier sea battle, and the indiscriminate use of terror against civilian populations in ways not seen since the Thirty Years War. Nuclear and incendiary bombs erased entire cities. V weapons brought new horror from the skies: the V1 with their hideous grumbling engines, the V2 with sudden, unexpected death. People were systematically starved: in Britain food had to be rationed because of the stranglehold of U-Boats, while in Holland the German blockage of food and fuel saw 30,000 die of starvation in the winter of 1944/5. It was a catastrophe for millions.

At a time of such enormous crisis, scientists sought ever more inventive weapons, or devices to help halt the war. Civilians were involved as never before, with women taking up new trades, proving themselves as capable as their male predecessors whether in the factories or the fields.

The stories in this book are of courage, of ingenuity, of hilarity in some cases, or of great sadness, but they are all thought-provoking - and rather weird. So whether you are interested in the last Polish cavalry charge, the Blackout Ripper, Dada, or Ghandi's attempt to stop the bloodshed, welcome to the Weirder War Two!

Click Bait
By Gillian Philip

A funny joke's a funny joke. Eddie Doolan doesn't think twice about adapting it to fit a tragic local news story and posting it on social media.

It's less of a joke when his drunken post goes viral. It stops being funny altogether when Eddie ends up jobless, friendless and ostracized by the whole town of Langburn. This isn't how he wanted to achieve fame.

Under siege from the press, and facing charges not just for the joke but for a history of abusive behavior on the internet, Eddie grows increasingly paranoid and desperate. The only people still speaking to him are Crow, a neglected kid who relies on Eddie for food and company, and Sid, the local gamekeeper's granddaughter. It's Sid who offers Eddie a refuge and an understanding ear.

But she also offers him an illegal shotgun - and as Eddie's life spirals downwards, and his efforts at redemption are thwarted at every turn, the gun starts to look like the answer to all his problems.

**Burning Bridges
By Chris Bedell**

They've always said that three's a crowd...

24-year-old Sasha didn't anticipate her identical twin Riley killing herself upon their reconciliation after years of estrangement. But Sasha senses an opportunity and assumes Riley's identity so she can escape her old life.

Playing Riley isn't without complications, though. Riley's had a strained relationship with her wife and stepson so Sasha must do whatever she can to make her newfound family love and accept her. If Sasha's arrangement ends, then she'll have nothing protecting her from her past. However, when one of Sasha's former clients tracks her down, Sasha must choose between her new life and the only person who cared about her.

But things are about to become even more complicated, as a third sister, Katrina, enters the scene...